J SmI

Smith

Edge of the forest.

9212

AN EDGE OF THE FOREST

Date Due

NOV 16 '59	JUN 4 '88	JAN 0 2 1996	
JAN 4 '60			
JUN 1 '61			
MY 24			
OCT 22 '62			
JAN 30 '63			
FEB 4 '63			
NO 12 '63			
MR 4 '64			
OCT 3 '64			
OCT 31 '66			
JA 12 '67			
JAN 2 '68			
5/27/18			

An EDGE
of the FOREST

by AGNES SMITH

DECORATIONS BY ROBERTA MOYNIHAN

NEW YORK · THE VIKING PRESS

J

10-23-59

Printed in the U. S. A. by the Vail-Ballou Press, Inc.

*For saints,
philosophers,
and artists;
and for M.*

THE FOREST

There is in this round world a very old country, so old it has forgotten its name, if indeed it ever had a name. An ocean is on one side of it. Mountains are on the other side, their tops so high that a few snowflakes fallen there long ago never melted. They fell into a windless place shaded from the sun, and they are the oldest things in that old country.

Almost as old as the snowflakes is a forest, called by the people of the country The Young Woods or The Children's Grove. Why an old and large forest, wild, far from the cities and towns of the country, is called by two such unfitting names, the people have forgotten. They seldom wonder about the names.

But children in the first years of school sometimes point delighted forefingers at a map, or cloud clear brows over a paragraph and exclaim, "How young is The Young Woods?" or, "What children does that grove belong to?" The teachers answer, but since no one really knows, the answers are never satisfactory, and the children who ask the questions are disturbed to discover that there are things grown persons do not understand either.

More rarely, in college, still-curious young people determine to trace down the names. They are not discouraged to learn from their professors that other students have tried to do this and failed. They read books. They write papers. A few of them travel the difficult journey to The Young Woods and talk to elderly persons who live near the forest. Old men and women are glad to tell the students everything their grandparents' grandparents said about the forest and its names, but none of them reveals why the old forest is called The Young Woods or The Children's Grove.

Whatever the reason for its name, the forest covers hundreds of miles of that country. In some parts the trees make a green sky which seems hardly lower than the blue sky above them. Streams wide and narrow run through it. There are rocky and marshy places, hills and valleys and plains. There are even grassy clearings, green bowls full of hot sunlight or cool dark. Of course there are young trees, too, and bushes, and the most delicate of ferns and flowers. But it is not a young woods. It is an old forest.

No children live in it. The families who live near do not feel it is their children's grove. The forest is old and large and wild. Their children are young and small and weak.

There are old stories about the old forest that have grown like trees, told by no one or told by everyone, of happenings as remote from the people who tell or listen to the stories as the forest itself is remote from their cities and towns. This is one of those old stories, not about the whole forest but only a small part of it, an edge of the forest.

AN EDGE OF THE FOREST

PART ONE

I

Once upon a time, during the early days of summer, in an edge of The Young Woods near the grasslands, a leopardess was lying in a patch of pale sunlight, watching her three kittens play. Her golden eyes were half closed. Dry brown leaves were beneath her. The lemon-colored sun was above her. She was gorged with meat, and her tongue remembered the warm taste and texture of antelope. The bellies of her kittens were round with rabbit; it amused her to watch their fierce play.

That day, with little help from their mother, they had found, stalked, and killed their own game. They had learned quickly to hunt. Their play no longer made their mother purr and tremble; she saw that soon she need not worry about them: they could take care of themselves.

At this thought the leopardess stretched, laid down her head, and closed her eyes. She listened to the wind. Her lair was in a sheltered cleft in a hillside, and the air around her hardly stirred, but above, in the tops of the trees, the wind played as fiercely as her kittens. Flowing in violent waves from the west, it broke itself against the hills and the trees. It made a sound in the sky as soft as the leopardess's purr. In the trees it snarled and spat and squealed like the kittens as they crouched and leaped and wrestled with one another. The trees groaned and swayed. Twigs and weak branches cracked, split, and clittered to earth.

The leopardess looked toward the treetops. The black kitten, who had been pretending to kill her yellow brother, sprang backward, away from him. She landed on her mother's paws. The paws at once clasped the kitten and the leopardess gave the struggling body a few licks with her rough tongue.

That one of her kittens was black had troubled the leopardess at first. She had seen black leopards, but she had been perturbed when her own white and spotted-yellow-ness had formed a kitten so extremely and entirely black. But the black kitten behaved exactly like the others, and her mother ceased to be troubled. Nevertheless, the leopardess did wash her more often than the yellow two. She paid more attention to her. She may even have loved her a little more.

The black kitten loved her mother dearly, but she could not help feeling she was bathed too often and too long. She was thinking this as her mother licked her, when her yellow sister padded toward their mother and began to play with her tail, pretending it was a snake. This annoyed the leopardess. She pinned the black kitten to the ground with one paw and turned to cuff and snarl at her yellow daughter. The black one saw her chance to escape. She gave a sudden wriggle, pushing her mother's paw aside with her hind legs, rolled over three times, and scurried away.

It was as she leaped toward her favorite hiding place, a hollow below a rock into which she fitted like an egg in its shell, that the dreadful thing happened. The wind, with a sound like thunder, split, like a flash of lightning, the trunk of a tree growing on the edge of the bank above the leopardess. The noise made the yellow kittens stiff with terror. Their mother tried to carry one and push the other out of the way, but they were all crushed by the trunk of the tree as it lurched down the bank.

Under the rock the black kitten heard the crunch and thud of the tree's fall. The rock saved her life, but the end of a broken branch scraped down the side of the rock and crushed her right front paw.

After a long time she pulled her paw loose. She whimpered and shivered as she licked it. A long time later, holding the swollen paw against her chest, she began to work her way through the wreckage of the tree.

The paw healed. It was flatter than the left paw. The curved claws would not slip all the way into their sheaths. It was stiff in the wrist.

A year later the young black leopardess moved through The Children's Grove as gracefully as any of her kind but with a sidewise gait and a slight lowering of her right shoulder as her weight fell on that paw. The even limp, the slanted motion, were not awkward, but seemed to make her strength and beauty easier to see, as though in teaching herself to use her crippled paw she had gained other strengths and beauties without losing those which are the inheritance of all leopards.

And she was a small leopardess. The death of her mother before she was quite ready to take care of herself, as well as her crushed paw, had made the first part of her life difficult. She had almost starved as the paw healed. Later, as she learned to hunt, she had nearly crippled herself again because she had been so desperate for meat that in the excitement of the hunt she forgot her crippled paw and tried to use it as though it were as strong as the other. But little by little the muscles of her narrow body learned to work with the flat paw. The pain and hunger of her first year had made the black leopardess smaller than other leopards, but they had made her wiser.

The fire in her light eyes was quiet and strong. In spite of her size and her paw, she was a most clever hunter. Young as she was, no other animals had tried to drive her from the part of The Children's Grove which was her home. When they appeared she pointed her blunt head and the shaft of her body at them, stared with her pale bright eyes, and they went away. They were not afraid of her but—they went away.

The Children's Grove, they thought as they turned aside, is large enough for all of us, and more. Also, I believe I would prefer a home deeper in the forest. This hillside is too close to the edge of the forest and the homes of man. Let this be the home of that young black leopardess.

The leopardess had not really chosen her home. She had

moved away from her birthplace and from the bones of her mother and brother and sister, but not far away. Something held her there; she did not know what. She had never returned to the fallen tree, but sometimes she went slowly, pausing often, within sight of the topmost dead twigs. At this distance she would make a circle around the place, her head lifted higher than she usually carried it, her movements less graceful than usual. She would make this wide circle exactly to the point she had started it. She would stand still a moment. Then, with a soft snarl deep in her throat, she would shoot off through the forest in a burst of exquisite speed, and finally she would go to her lair and sleep. The leopardess's lair was farther down the hillside, nearer the grasslands than her mother's had been; and it was under the roots of an enormous tree.

The tree had begun its life five hundred years before in a pocket of earth on a ledge of rock. Now the rock was clasped by the roots of the tree as a stone is grasped by a hand. The leopardess went through a screen of branchlike roots before she saw the low entrance of her cave. The cave was large and dry, with a soft floor of sandy soil.

The hillside was a long gentle slope with outcroppings of stone, inhabited by tremendous trees with high delicate foliage. Here and there, upward from the leopardess's lair, were a few groups of lower trees and bushes. Downward, the forest gradually changed its appearance. Shorter trees with heavier foliage grew more closely together. The undergrowth thickened. At the foot of the hill's slope in a tangle of willows and other water-loving trees, reeds, and grasses, flowed a broad shallow river. On the other side of the river, beyond a swampy thicket, the grasslands began.

In winter when the leaves had fallen from the trees there were gaps in the treetops through which the leopardess could see, far away through the empty air over the grasslands, a thread of smoke rising from one of the homes of man. A narrow lace of treetops also showed above the rolling horizon there. It was the home of a shepherd.

The leopardess noticed the smoke without curiosity, as part of her landscape. She knew it was a home of man. She was born knowing that man lives in the world, but the home was too far away to concern her. She had never seen man. The shepherd's flocks had not for years grazed near The Young Woods. The shepherd had more fields than he needed; the sheep strayed into the forest if they were near it, or they were preyed upon by the forest animals. He kept his flocks away from The Young Woods.

The leopardess did half her hunting in The Children's Grove and half along the river and in the grasslands. She liked the dense thickets, the damp coolness of the river. Often after she had eaten well she would stretch herself upon the broad branch of an old willow which grew on the riverbank down the slope of the hill from her cave. The river's bed was rocky there and the water sang and sparkled. There she would rest and doze, listen to all the watery sounds of the place and sniff the moist smells. It was especially pleasant in the heat of summer.

It was there, but in the early days of spring, that the black leopardess and the black lamb began their friendship.

2

The leopardess and the lamb would never have met if it had not been for a half-grown, half-crazy dog.

He belonged, as did the mother of the lamb, to the shepherd whose chimney smoke and orchard could be seen from the edge of the forest. The shepherd had large flocks and needed many sheep dogs to guard them as they grazed. He and his father and his father's father had bred their own dogs, and they were the finest of the country. Shepherds came from far away to buy them after he had trained them, and the shepherd's training was as fine as the dogs themselves. A dog trained by this shepherd was almost as useful as a man or woman in caring for a flock of sheep.

When the dog of this story was born, the daughter of the shepherd—his youngest child and only daughter—took him early from his mother and made an especial pet of him. He was a funny, handsome puppy and the little girl loved him.

She spoiled him. He was not only allowed to come into the house, which was forbidden to the other dogs, but he also slept under her bed and was given bones and scraps from her plate. The shepherd knew that these were bad habits for a sheep dog, and he told his daughter so, but she liked having the puppy with her so much, and the shepherd was so fond of his little girl, that the puppy lived in the house until he was grown.

When he became large and strong and wildly playful the little girl did not like so much to have him in the house!

He knocked over furniture. He tore up rugs and shoes and one of her best dresses. When he jumped against her to show his love he almost unbalanced her, and one day as she was giving him a bone he snatched at it so quickly that one of his teeth tore her hand. The little girl saw then that her father was right about the dog and that he should live in the kennels with the other sheep dogs.

At that time he was of an age when the shepherd began to train the young dogs to guard the sheep. The shepherd took him with the others to the grasslands for his training. The shepherd was a kind man. He liked dogs and understood them, but his training was difficult and used a great deal of patience. It was twice as difficult for the spoiled young dog as for the others. And, too, the other dogs were jealous of him because he was a pet and had not lived long in the kennels. They snarled and snapped at him when the shepherd was not with them. The young dog became unhappy. He learned slowly. The shepherd was more patient with him than with any of the rest, but he soon saw that the poor dog was too spoiled to be well trained and decided that he should be killed.

The shepherd's daughter heard of this. She ran to her father and with tears begged him not to kill her pet. Her father told her that it would be best for the dog to die, that he would be unhappy, that he might even become a bad dog. Hearing this, the little girl cried more bitterly, and so her father said, "Well, my dear, perhaps we can make a watchdog of him. I'll wait a while to see how he develops. He may improve and settle down, but don't be too hopeful."

Now the dog was half-trained, as well as spoiled and un-happy and disliked. It was not his fault that he developed badly. He often fought with other dogs. In trying to be friendly he made himself a nuisance around the house and he began to wander alone through the grasslands and to show a peculiar interest in the sheep. He was badly chewed up in a fight when he frightened some of the sheep an older dog was guarding. Herdsmen beat and shamed him when he bothered them. Even the little girl, his best friend, often spoke sharply when he tried to play with her.

To his sorrow and ignorance was added fear and slyness and hate of everything. His heart was broken.

3

The mother of the black lamb was a young ewe as white as skimmed milk in winter. Her wool was the pride of the shepherd and the envy of the other ewes.

The black lamb was the first lamb she had had, and she was proud but nervous. It was the only black lamb in her flock. She could not understand why it was so black and she so white. When the shepherd's third son first saw it he had laughed and picked it up in his arms and held it against his face. "Ah," he had said. "Ah!" he had sighed. "This one is my own." The ewe had been pleased, but she had been more puzzled than ever: the shepherd's third son had not picked up any other lamb of her flock. She looked at the whiteness of the other lambs, and although she did not love her own lamb less because it was black, she worried about it more. She stayed as far away from the rest of her flock as the shepherd's son and his dog would let her. When her lamb went to play with the other lambs she called it back to her.

The ewes soon noticed her strange behavior. They began to think she was too proud of her lamb because it was black and because the shepherd had picked it up. They were already a little jealous because of the young ewe's beautiful wool, and when she seemed to consider her lamb too good to play with their lambs, they drove the black one away from them and would not let their lambs play with her.

The lambs were still far too young and too busy learning how to walk on their long legs to notice what was going on among their mothers. The black lamb noticed a little. She had no one to play with and more time to notice such things, but she loved her beautiful white mother and liked to be with her. She played by herself.

Sometimes, though, she was lonely. Once she tried to play with a rabbit. The rabbit looked at her with surprise. She went closer, and the rabbit was angry. It said something the lamb could not quite understand, but she thought it was, "Oh, my! Have even lambs begun to eat us now? You see if you can catch me!" The rabbit was gone so quickly that the lamb could hardly believe a rabbit had ever been there. She shook her head sadly and went back to her mother.

What would have become of the black lamb if she had continued to live such a lonely life with her mother's flock can never be known. Her childhood with the flock ended just as she had learned to use her legs for short jumps and the simplest of capers.

In his roving from flock to flock over the shepherd's fields the spoiled dog discovered that the ewe and her black lamb grazed always at the edge of the flock, or far ahead of it or behind it. By now he had learned well that if a shepherd or a sheep dog saw him he would be shamed and driven away, and so he watched the ewe and her lamb, but he was careful that no one watched him.

To see those two, almost alone, filled the half-crazed head and the broken heart of the young dog with queer thoughts and twisted feelings. He lay for a whole day in the grass, his head on his paws, and watched them. He took his eyes off them only to guard himself against discovery by the shepherd's son and his dog.

The next day he watched them so closely that he did not see what caused the flock to scatter. There was a sudden rush of noise. The ewes and the lambs ran in all directions, crying with fright. The shepherd's third son shouted and ran. The old sheep dog barked so fiercely and ran so fast, he sounded as though he were three dogs instead of one.

Neither the ewe nor the black lamb saw what had frightened the flock, but the sounds of fright terrified them. They ran blindly away, farther and farther away from the flock.

The young dog ran with them, ran just behind them.

They ran a long distance before the ewe noticed where they were going. The sounds of the flock were faint. The ewe was tired and stopped to look around. She saw the tall reeds and grasses and low trees of a brook. She thought it a good place to hide until the flock was quiet and led the lamb to a clump of dwarf willows where they would be hidden, but she was uneasy. She could hardly hear the flock or the shouts of the shepherd's son or the barking of the sheep dog.

She went to the brook for a drink. She told her lamb not to be frightened, that as soon as they had rested they would return to the flock. The grass growing along the brook was sweet. The ewe ate a little of it as she rested. The lamb looked at the brook and listened to the water murmuring its way through the reeds. They were glad to rest.

The ewe did not know how much time had passed when first she noticed that she could no longer hear any sounds of the flock. She lifted her head high to listen, and all she could hear was the murmur of the brook and the swish of the breezes in the grass. A little fire of fear began to burn in her heart.

"Come, come!" she said to her lamb. "We must go back now."

She turned to start up the grassy bank, and the spoiled young dog growled at her out of a clump of dried reeds. "No!" his growl said. "Go down the brook! Go!"

The flame of fear in the ewe's heart became a roaring fire of confusion. This was not the dog which guarded her flock; but he was a sheep dog. She did not know what to do. She stood still, feeling her lamb close beside her.

"Go," the dog growled. "Turn and go!"

He slunk toward them through the grass. The ewe saw

his crazed eyes, his frothy tongue drooling out of his mouth. She heard the heat and thickness of his voice. Her fear smothered her, but the touch of her lamb kept her mind clear. She thought, I will go up the bank. At the top I will be able to see the flock. Maybe the shepherd's son and his dog are looking for us now. I will call to them.

But when she started up the bank the dog growled at her, "No! Go down the brook!" He went up the bank above her and growled again.

The ewe could think of nothing to do but turn down the brook. She kept herself between her lamb and the dog. She tried to go slowly, but the dog would not allow this. He snapped at her heels until she and her lamb were trotting down the brook.

He kept them at a trot until they could go no farther, and then the ewe turned to face the dog. He will kill me, she thought, but I will call to the shepherd before I die and he and his good dog will find my lamb before she is hurt.

But the dog only stretched himself out on the grass and stared at the ewe with his red eyes. After she had rested, the dog growled at her again, "Go on! Go on!" And this time he made them run faster.

And so they ran and rested, and ran and rested, until the ewe and her lamb were too tired to be afraid. They ached with weariness. Their chests burned with their breathing. Their eyes saw only a fog of grass. At last, though, the ewe looked up as they stopped to rest, and looming above her through the haze of her weariness was the tall rise of a hill, the green gloom of trees. She saw an edge of the forest.

The young ewe despaired. "Come to me," she said to her lamb. "I must die now. The mad dog has driven us to The Young Woods. My grandmother has told me about The Young Woods. Death lives there, and not one death only, but a thousand deaths. I should have called to the shepherd and died in the beginning, and he would have heard me and run to you. I will die now and you must try to go back along the brook until you find the flock. I hope the mad dog will forget you after he has killed me. And now farewell, my own lamb, my first one, my black one. Do not be afraid. I am sure the shepherd will find you. Go back from me now. Close your eyes while I am dying. Then run."

The lamb stepped backward until she was behind her mother. She closed her eyes.

4

The young black leopardess was happy. She had had a good hunt. All morning she had followed deer through the forest. She liked best to hunt deer, to look at them as well as eat them, and often, even when she was hungry, she looked at them a long time before she killed one. Occasionally she startled them and let them run so that she could stalk and watch them again.

She always killed deer quickly, so quickly that they were dead before they had time to be afraid. She had learned through watching and hunting deer that to be afraid is one thing and that to be afraid to die is another. To be afraid is often useful. To be afraid to die is always useless. When she had learned this, something was healed that had been hurt in her heart when her paw was crippled. The day she had learned about fear and death she had said, "Now I know myself, and now I am well and happy."

Today the leopardess had killed a yearling buck so quickly that he had not lifted his head from the new grass before he died, and she had seen his friends soar away among the trees, afraid and free. She had purred to watch them.

The trouble was, she had eaten too much of the meat before she dragged what was left of it up a tree and hung it between trunk and branch to keep until she was hungry again. She had thought she would stay in that grassy glade until she had finished eating her kill, but now she decided she would not soon be hungry and she thought of her broad willow branch over the river below her hillside.

She went there. She slept.

She had not slept long enough when she was awakened. She raised her head and stretched her left front paw. She yawned. She was not glad to be awake.

She put down her head, stretched her right hind leg, and tried to sleep again, but the strange sounds that had wakened her kept her awake. She looked up the river, where a brook from the grasslands emptied into it, and she waited to see what was making the sounds. As she waited and listened, the fur prickled on the back of her neck and along her spine. She forgot sleeping. The tip of her tail twitched. She did not like what she heard.

Soon the leopardess saw two animals she had never seen before, and they were acting in a way she had never seen other animals act. She always looked at strange things, whether she liked them or not, and so she lay still and watched.

One of the animals did not puzzle her. He was a fox-wolf animal. He was too large to be a fox and his fur was longer than a wolf's and another color, and his talk was a little different, but it was fox-wolf talk.

He was mad, that strange fox-wolf. As she saw and thought this the leopardess's small ears flattened against her head and her long fangs suddenly gleamed white against her red throat. She was born knowing about madness and she knew it was fearful, but she had never seen it before, and the sight made her tongue curl in her throat with sick horror.

The other animal puzzled her. She was glad to stop looking at the fox-wolf and look at the other animal because, although it was tired and hurt, it was not mad. It was as black as she, but its fur grew in little whorls. She could tell it was young because its head was too large and its legs were too long for its body. She tried to remember another animal it resembled. It was a little, but only a little, like a new-born deer. At least, it had hoofs, not paws.

Both the fox-wolf and the black young animal were bloody and unclean. The leopardess could smell them as they came down the river. Her fangs gleamed again and her tail lashed.

The madness of the fox-wolf was a strange madness, a kind of madness she was not born knowing about. He seemed to want to kill the young animal, but he did not kill

it. He made it run and fall, and then he snarled and snapped
at it until it got up and stumbled on a few steps and fell
again. When the young black animal fell it turned its blood-
smeared face to the mad fox-wolf and said something. The
leopardess could not understand what it said at first. Even-
tually she did understand. It was saying, "Kill me. Let me
die. Kill me."

Again horror curled the leopardess's tongue and flattened
her ears. Her crippled paw pressed against her chest. The
stench of madness and death was so strong in her throat that
it choked her. She shivered.

But as the two strange animals came their strange way
down the river the leopardess crept farther out on her willow
branch and crouched there. She thought, This must not
come into The Children's Grove. I have to kill it. It will
make me sick, but I have to kill it.

She leaped from her branch, broke the fox-wolf's neck,
and, choking and moaning through her teeth, dragged his
body far out into the grasslands and dropped it into a bog
of slimy water.

Then she was very sick.

After that was over she felt better, but she scurried to the
edge of the forest as she used to scurry under her rock when
she was a kitten, with anxious leaps, as fast as she could go.

5

When she reached the river the leopardess did a thing she
had never done before. She went to a deep pool below a

waterfall and jumped into it. She swam until she felt clean, until the stench of the mad fox-wolf was gone from her nose and mouth. Then she climbed out of the pool and gave herself a second bath with her tongue.

She thought of sleep again and went to her willow tree.

She was surprised to find the black animal still lying where it had fallen when she had killed the fox-wolf. She had thought it would go away, but it seemed to have died there. Now she would have to carry it to the bog too, and take another bath. She did not want dead things near her willow tree. She hated to touch madness and death again, but she crossed the river and approached the little thing.

It was alive. It opened its eyes and looked at her. It tried to stand and could not, but it held up its head, although it nodded with weakness, and said, "Kill me. Let me die."

The leopardess sat down. She did not notice but she held her crippled paw against her chest as she stared at the young animal. "I am not hungry," she said.

The lamb closed her eyes.

The leopardess could not understand what she was seeing and hearing. At last she said, "Are you so afraid of death that you have died alive?"

The lamb did not speak, but she opened her eyes and the leopardess could see in them that she was not afraid of death. There was no fear of any kind in those tired eyes.

Again the leopardess thought a long time before she spoke. "You are a young animal," she said. "You do not know what you are saying— 'Kill me, let me die.' Where is your mother, that you were alone with madness and have learned to speak such old words with your milky mouth?"

The lamb did not move or make a sound. She was not listening to the leopardess and she could hardly have understood her if she had been listening. She felt the damp cool air going in and out of her chest. She heard her heart beating. She thought, They are working hard, as though they were the chest and the heart of someone else.

But as the leopardess said "your mother," something seemed to waken the lamb from her weariness, and she knew that it was her own chest and heart she felt. She looked into the pale eyes of the leopardess. "Is this The Children's Grove?" she asked.

She heard the strange voice say, "Yes."

The lamb sighed and lifted her head. "My mother said before she died that death lives in The Children's Grove, and not one death only, but a thousand deaths. She hoped the mad dog would forget me after he had killed her, but he did not forget me. Now I am in The Children's Grove. Are you death?"

As she asked her question the leopardess's light eyes closed and her sleek head jerked away from the lamb, as though the question had been a blow. When she spoke, her voice was so soft that the lamb could hardly hear it.

"No. I am not death. I am only a young black leopardess," she said. "What are you?"

The lamb felt sleep in her bones, warm and sweet as her mother's milk. She could not open her eyes but she heard her voice say, "I am a black lamb."

She slept.

6

The leopardess crossed the river to her willow branch, but now she was wide awake. She made herself comfortable, with her head turned so she could see the sleeping lamb, and she rested and watched the lamb and thought.

First she remembered everything that had happened. Next she wondered why it had happened. Why were the mad fox-wolf and the black lamb strange to her? She had wandered days and miles over the grasslands and she had supposed she knew all those animals. She remembered everything she could of the grasslands, and soon she thought of the smoke and the lace of trees on the horizon, and she said to herself, They must be man's animals.

Then there came into her mind a story her mother had told her when she was a kitten, about how, when her mother was younger, she had gone close to man's homes to hunt—dog? Yes, dog was the name of the man's animal her mother had hunted. The black lamb had said dog. The leopardess decided she did not like dogs. Certainly not when they were mad.

The only other man's animals she remembered hearing her mother mention were—flocksheep, she thought it was, and calf. She had had an idea, when she was a kitten, that a flocksheep was a large white animal, almost too large to think about, and soft, somehow, like feathers or moss. All she could remember about calf was its name and that it was man's.

Nowhere in all her memory could she find a black lamb or anything like a black lamb. Perhaps it was not one of man's animals, after all?

The leopardess stared across the river at the lamb. Often it shivered and trembled in its sleep, and sighed and breathed heavily. It was lying on rock, close to the river. It had been too tired to find a better place.

The leopardess had never seen anything so tired. "Kill me," it had said, "let me die." She arched her neck and closed her eyes as she remembered how it had asked, "Are you death?" Something hurt in her heart and winced in her head that had never hurt or winced before.

She closed her eyes and wished she could sleep. She did sleep.

The moon was shining when she wakened. She looked first at the lamb and saw that it was still asleep. Then, as was her habit, she looked at everything she could see, listened to everything she could hear, and smelled everything she could smell. She saw and heard nothing unusual, but she could smell death strongly, the clotted blood on the black lamb, the blood of its mother.

The leopardess thought, This lamb will die soon enough. The hunters of death will smell her out.

She no sooner thought this than she heard the laughter of the hyenas, the hunters of death. She had no sooner heard that laughter from the grasslands than she saw a shadowy hyena-shape run through the shadows across the river. It paused there, ran into the moonlight a few steps, then ran back and was a shadow again.

Slowly the leopardess rose and stood on the willow branch. She began to breathe deep breaths. Her eyes and her head followed precisely the shadow moving through the shadows across the river. Slowly her flat sides stretched outward until the curve of each rib could be seen under the shimmering fur. Slowly her sides flattened until the big muscles of her shoulders and flanks seemed to be held together only by the ridge of her backbone.

Out of the shadows across the river came a shadowy sound, a kind of chuckle. This ceased and the shadow left the shadows and darted to the lamb. The laughter began. The ugly face pointed toward the moon and the greasy laughter spread and splattered.

The leopardess coughed. The harsh sound rasped and hacked the night. She screamed, and the sound seemed to split and shatter and blast the dark air. That edge of The Young Woods became as quiet as the moon above it. She screamed again, and far out on the grasslands the laughter of the hyenas faded. Across the river the shadow in the shadows had vanished.

Once more the leopardess coughed, and the silence became like silence dead and frozen. Only the lamb moved. She staggered out of sleep. She stumbled a few steps into the shallow water of the river, and there she too was still, in the center of the silence.

The lamb did not hear the leopardess leap from her branch. She saw only her eyes, as pale and bright as the moon, suddenly shining across the river. Then she heard the strange-familiar voice.

"Come over here," said the leopardess. "Come into The Children's Grove. The river is shallow here. It will hardly wet your hoofs. You can rest here. Will you come?"

The lamb was very black and very small, standing in the center of the wide silence, in the clear light of the young spring moon, above the glittering silver of the river, at the edge of the forest. She turned her head toward the grass-lands. She bent to the river and wet her nose and mouth. She looked toward the leopardess.

"I will come," she said.

7

The leopardess stepped into the river to meet the lamb. She said, "Black Lamb, you must wash off the blood of your mother and the stench of madness that clings to your fur where the fox-wolf slavered on you. That hunter of death has left this edge of the forest forever, but tomorrow another may pass this way."

"It was death that wakened me," said the lamb. "I heard the voice of death."

The leopardess flexed her crippled paw and licked the fur on her right shoulder before she spoke. "No," she said, "that was not the voice of death that wakened you. Can you think of nothing but death?"

The lamb trembled. "My mother is dead," she said. "I am alone."

The leopardess shook the water off her crippled paw and put it back in the river. She did not look at the lamb as she spoke. "My mother, too, died while I needed her," she said.

There was a long silence.

"Do you want me to wash myself in the river?" the lamb asked. "The water is cold."

"Death is colder," said a voice from a branch close above their heads.

The lamb swirled away from the voice and fell into the water. The splash of her fall scattered beads of water all over the leopardess and she leaped sideways to a rock and shook herself and rubbed her eyes.

"Ah, me," said the voice. "I wish I could laugh."

The lamb did not attempt to get up. She whispered to the leopardess, "Is that death?"

The leopardess licked her whiskers impatiently. "No," she said. "That is an old owl. Pay no attention to him. He talks too much."

"Roll yourself over," said the voice. "Kick up a spray. What you cannot avoid, you may as well enjoy."

"Shall I pay attention to him?" the lamb asked the leopardess.

"No," said the leopardess. "But roll yourself over."

The lamb rolled herself over and over and over. The water was cold, but it felt good after she was used to it. She kicked her little black hoofs and wriggled her ears and her tail, and she puffed through her nose into the water. "Ha!" she said and rolled herself over again. She stood up and looked for the leopardess.

The leopardess was as still as the stone she was on.

"Is that enough?" the lamb asked, but even as she spoke,

her weakness came back into her and she fell to her knees in the water. "Aaah," she said, and the black of the night and the silver of the moon and the water whirled like a wind. Then she felt soft wings beating her head and something sharp plucked at her ears. She heard a close swoop of wings, and the voice of the old owl screeched to the leopardess, "Pick it up by the back of its neck and carry it out of the water! I may talk too much, but my mother is as dead as yours, you ineffable idiot!"

The lamb managed to stand up.

The leopardess limped toward her through the water. "Pay no attention to that bird," she said. "He talks too much, and he has only two legs. Even those two are not legs: they are twigs from a tree. Are you better now?"

"I am better now," said the lamb.

"The river is broad here, but it is shallow all the way across. Then there is a path through the bushes. We will go slowly and you can rest as we go. Will you come?"

The lamb breathed deeply. She shook herself. "I am coming," she said.

8

The lamb and the leopardess went up the hillside. The lamb was not used to paths, nor was she used to briars and bushes and branches or the nearness of night in the forest. On the grasslands and in the sheepfold with the flock night had been high and far away. Here night was low and close, as close as the flock had been. On the grasslands moonlight was another kind of day. In the forest the moonlight was part of the night, close and moving, but quiet.

The lamb was glad the leopardess was beside her. She was as quiet as the moonlight and as dark as the night; but, She is not death, the lamb thought, she is only a young black leopardess.

Little by little as they climbed the path the trees were farther apart, stood tall in the air, and held their branches higher. Night and the moonlight were still close and filled the forest, but they left enough room for the lamb and the leopardess. And now the old owl swooped and circled above them.

Often, especially when they rested, the owl talked to the leopardess, but the lamb was not used to his talk and could understand little of what he said. The leopardess paid no attention to the owl. The lamb tried not to notice him, but she could not help it. He was white, whiter than the moonlight, and the circles of his flight and the keen and clear quavering of his voice made her forget how tired she was as they went up the long hill. But the lamb's hoofs were sore. Her head felt too heavy for her neck and drooped lower and lower as she walked. She did not see the leopardess stop, but stumbled on.

The leopardess asked, "Where are you going?" and when the lamb turned she said, "Here is my home at the edge of the forest. I will be happy if you rest here until you find a place that is better for you."

The lamb tried to blink the sleep out of her eyes.

"Where?" she sighed and tottered after the leopardess through the roots of the tree. In the cave the ground was soft. The lamb fell upon it and seemed to melt into it. She was asleep before her eyes were closed.

The leopardess glanced around her cave and gazed at the lamb sleeping quietly and deeply before she went out of the cave.

The owl had alighted on the stub of a dead branch above the cave's entrance. The leopardess seemed not to see him. She went to a young tree and sharpened her claws. She lifted her head and sniffed the air. She returned to the front of the rock and looked up at the owl.

"Nothing will come tonight," she said, "but I wish you would stay here until I return. I will bring you food."

"You talk too much," said the owl.

"Good night, Owl," said the leopardess politely and went swiftly up the hillside, deeper into the forest.

The owl ruffled his feathers and preened them. He locked his talons on the dead branch. His round eyes slowly closed and opened, and closed, and opened. He stared at the moonlight.

Several moments later he said, "Ah, me," closed and opened his eyes, and stared at the moonlight again.

PART TWO

I

As day was dawning the leopardess returned, but she did not go directly to her cave; she had thought she heard an odd sound. She was carrying three baby rabbits, two dead and one alive. The dead ones she hung on a bush and, still carrying the other gently in her mouth, she walked about, observing her hillside. Everything seemed as usual. She picked the rabbits off the bush and went on.

She was in sight of the cave-rock when she heard the odd sound again, "Mah-eh-eh-eh!" It was not a loud cry, but the forest was so quiet in the dawn that it could be heard plainly. The leopardess crept closer. She came within sight of the cave and stopped and stared at what she saw.

In front of the cave stood the lamb, and standing on the ground in front of the lamb was the owl. The owl was talking rapidly and shifting from talon to talon as he talked.

Suddenly the lamb opened her mouth and said, "Mah-eh-eh-eh-eh!"

As she said this the owl flurried into the air, dropped to the ground, ruffled his feathers, and talked faster than before. The lamb gazed at him solemnly.

The leopardess went on to the cave. She put the rabbits

on the ground. The one still alive she held quiet under her flat paw. "What is the matter?" she asked.

The lamb and the owl both replied at once. The lamb said, "Mah-eh-eh-eh-eh! Mah-eh-eh!" The owl spiraled into the air and fluttered to the ground, saying, "I tell her and she listens to me and she agrees with me, but she doesn't stop."

"I can't help it," said the lamb. "I am hungry. Mah-eh. Mah-eh-eh-eh-eh!" The owl bounced into the air and the lamb said, "I'm sorry, Owl, but I can't help it. It comes out of my stomach before my head can stop it."

This time as he left the ground the owl snatched up one of the dead rabbits. Before he flew away with it he hovered over the leopardess and said, "Milk is what it wants, and milk is out of my sphere. I will do anything I can, but milk is beyond me."

"Mah-eh-eh-eh-eh-eh!" cried the lamb, and the owl was gone in a whirlwind of haste. "I can't help it," the lamb said sorrowfully to the leopardess. "I am hungry."

"What did your mother eat?" asked the leopardess.

"Grass."

"Never rabbits?"

"Never rabbits."

"Always grass?"

"Always grass," said the lamb. "Mah-eh-eh! I can't help it. I am so hungry."

The leopardess said, "Over there is a spring of water with grass growing around it. You will have to silence your stomach with those."

"Mah-eh-eh-eh!" said the lamb. "I can't help it. What has happened to the poor little rabbits?" she asked. She had just noticed them.

"They made too much noise," said the leopardess, "and death heard them."

The lamb began to cry, "Mah-eh-eh—" but she stopped. "Does death listen?" she asked.

"All the time," said the leopardess, "especially in The Children's Grove."

The lamb sighed. "Where is the water and the grass?" she asked.

"Over there. Do you see? You go ahead and I will follow in a moment."

As the lamb walked toward the spring the leopardess killed the third rabbit. She leaped to the top of the rock, climbed the tree, and hung the two dead rabbits on the owl's dead branch.

From high in the tree the owl said softly, "I pity you. I can't help it."

The leopardess dropped to the rock and washed her face.

A small well-cleaned bone fell from the top of the tree, and the owl spoke softly again. "This will be more difficult than a crushed paw. The lamb will be hungry a long time before she dies. She will make this edge of the forest dreadful with her cries. Then she will lie down and moan. Then she will be still. It would be better if you would kill her quickly, now."

The leopardess seemed not to have heard the owl. She finished washing her face and limped after the lamb. As the lamb drank water and chewed unhappily on a few blades of grass the leopardess took a nap.

The owl glided down around the trunk of the tree through the mists of morning. He picked the rabbits off the dead branch and carried them to the top of the tree. "Delicious!" he murmured to himself as he flew upward. "Delectable! I could not have made a better selection myself. Superb delicacy! The prime of succulence!"

The leopardess wakened from her nap. She rolled to her back, clawed the air with her forepaws, stretched, sat up, and yawned.

The lamb almost said, "Mah-eh-eh!" but she hurriedly nibbled some grass and washed it down with a sip of water. "I can see that someday I will like grass, and even water," she said to the leopardess, "but it does not make my stomach happy now. Milk always makes all of me very happy. Mah-eh— Oh, my!" The lamb took another quick bite of grass.

The leopardess licked her crippled paw. Then she reclined as though she were going to sleep. The lamb gazed at her sadly before she moved to a fresh patch of grass.

The leopardess was still lying limply on the ground when next she spoke, but she was looking at the lamb through half-opened eyes. "Black Lamb," she said, "if you take a large drink of water and go into the darkest corner of the cave and lie down, do you think you can rest? Will your stomach let you be quiet a while?"

"Why?" the lamb asked.

"I am going to leave you, and the owl is asleep. If you are

quiet I think you will be safe. If you cry I do not know what may happen."

"Death?" whispered the lamb.

The leopardess arose and shook herself. "You make my fur prickle when you say that. Try to think of something else."

"What may happen if I cry?" asked the lamb, after she had tried to think of something else.

"Death," said the leopardess, and she shook herself again. "Will you try to be quiet?"

"I will try to be quiet." The lamb drank as much water as she could and walked slowly toward the cave.

"I will return as soon as I can," said the leopardess.

The lamb looked back. "I will be happy to see you come," she said, "because you are only a young black leopardess."

"Yes," said the leopardess. She shook herself yet again before she started off through the forest.

She returned a long time later, very tired. She found the lamb asleep in the cave. She came out of the cave and looked toward the top of the tree.

The owl said, "I am awake."

"I will rest until the sun is low," said the leopardess, "and then, if you will help me, we will bring some milk to the black lamb."

"I thought I was awake," said the owl. "What did you say?"

The leopardess leaped to the top of the rock, arranged herself on some dried leaves between two roots of the tree, and went to sleep.

The owl stretched one wing and one leg. He closed his eyes, but after a short nap he awakened, opening and closing his eyes and stepping sidewise up and down his perch.

"Milk," he said, "milk." He stood very still. "I believe I had better eat another rabbit, quickly."

He ate another rabbit, quickly.

Before the leopardess awakened, the lamb came out of the cave crying "M—m-m-m-! M-m-m!" with her mouth closed. She trotted up and down near the cave and then ran to the spring and the grass. The owl floated like a large snowflake from the top of the tree, and he alighted, without a whisper of sound, on the lowest branch of a tree near the spring.

"For such a young one you do well," he said. "Eat and drink as much and as fast as you can. Strange things are about to happen, and the less one has in one's stomach the stranger strange things are."

The lamb choked on her grass blade. "I would be happier," she said when she could speak, "if I would see you before you talk to me. You are too soon after nothing."

"I beg you to forgive me," said the owl. "I will try to remember, henceforward, to be visible to you before I am audible; but old habits are hard to break." After he said this the owl closed his eyes. "Milk," he said to himself. "Milk."

"Mah-eh-eh-eh-eh-eh-eh-eh-eh-eh!" cried the lamb mournfully, with all her heart.

The leopardess sprang spitting and clawing out of her sleep. She climbed twice her height up the trunk of the tree before she turned her head to see what had wakened her. She looked first into the eyes of the owl, who was by then sitting on his dead branch over the entrance to the leopardess's cave.

"Milk," said the owl.

The leopardess saw the lamb standing by the spring. She dropped to the rock and bit out a piece of bark that was caught in one of her claws. She went to the spring and drank water. "Eat as much as you can," she said to the lamb, "and quickly. You must go into the cave and be quiet again. I hope this evening your stomach will be happier."

"That is what the owl told me to do," said the lamb, "and that is what I was doing, but then he said— Mah-eh-eh!"

"Eat some grass," urged the leopardess. "Drink some water. Pay no attention to the owl. He talks too much."

The lamb said, "Even when I pay attention to him I understand only a little of what he says. But I like him. He is not death. He is only a white owl, even when he is here before he comes."

" 'Even when he—' Oh. You will soon be used to that," said the leopardess. "Eat quickly. The owl and I must go."

The lamb ate quickly but not much. She said, "My stomach is sad now. All it wants is to be quiet," and she went to the darkest corner of the cave and bent herself around her stomach. "I couldn't help it," she said to her stomach. "You were so hungry and we have to be quiet."

The owl flew to the low branch near the spring and the leopardess talked to him.

The owl thought.

"If it is probable," he said. "It should be possible. But, black one, why do you do this?"

"Because this is what I wish to do," the leopardess interrupted, "and there is no time to talk about it. Will you go?"

"Of course I will go with you," said the owl, "but it is dangerous to break old habits, and—"

The leopardess had started swiftly across the slope of the hill and the owl had to hurry to catch up with her. He flew above her head and went on talking as he flew. He hoped the leopardess was listening to him, because what he had to say that evening was important; but he never could tell whether she was listening or not. He had reached the most important part of his talk when the leopardess stopped and looked at him. He circled slowly above her. He was pleased.

"I am glad you see that the sequence of events must of necessity lead to a recurrence of—" he began.

The leopardess did not allow him to finish. "She is over her fear now," she said, "but you must be quiet until the proper moment. She will be thinking about starting back, and any strange noise will send her off." The leopardess went on, not so swiftly, much more carefully.

The owl muttered to himself, " 'Any strange noise' indeed!" and flew after her.

2

In early dusk the leopardess and the owl approached a small clearing in the forest, near the top of a hill. There was a flat place backed by a shelf of bare rock, and a spring made a green pool before the water flowed down the hill. The tall trees stood back from the water and the rocks, and grass and ferns and bushes and short trees grew on and among the rocks and around the pool.

Before they had quite reached the clearing the leopardess stopped and the owl flew into the tops of the tall trees. From there he flew into the pool of air above the pool of water, back and forth, up and down, looking below him as though he were hunting. After a moment he folded his wings and plunged steeply down the air among the tall trees as though he had seen his prey. But he alighted on the ground near the leopardess, whispered to her while making scratching sounds in the dead leaves; and then he flew back into the clearing and circled and swooped as before.

Without cracking a dead twig on the ground or brushing a green leaf on a bush the leopardess moved through the quiet gloom, around a rock, across the brook below the pool, up a slant of rock, into a thicket of bushes. At the edge of the thicket was a group of small trees, and among these trees grew a sparse fine grass. A spotted fawn lay on the grass, and beside him grazed his mother.

The fawn was asleep, but the doe was tense with wakefulness. She glanced at her fawn, bent her head to the grass, snatched a mouthful, and raised her head to look and listen and smell. The flight of the owl interested her. She went toward the edge of the group of small trees to see him more clearly, and when, an instant later, she glanced at her fawn, the leopardess was standing above him.

The leopardess had been so quiet that the fawn had not awakened, although her head was close above his and her flat paw seemed to touch his shoulder.

The doe did not start or tremble. She did not even breathe quickly. It was as though, standing there, all of her had died, except her eyes. After her eyes had seen her sleeping fawn under the paw of the leopardess she looked at the eyes of the leopardess. Then it was as though the leopardess had died standing there too, except her eyes. The brown eyes and the yellow eyes stared into each other.

The doe whispered, "What?" The leopardess had not spoken and still she did not speak, but the doe whispered again, "What?"

The owl alighted on the ground in front of the doe and began at once to talk. The doe saw her fawn awaken, saw the leopardess lean forward, holding the fawn against the ground, and after a moment during which neither the leopardess nor the fawn moved, the doe listened to the owl.

Only when the owl had finished what he had to say did she look at him. "Yes," she said. "I will."

But after she had spoken she began to quiver. All of a sudden she ceased to quiver and, with a great smooth leap, she was off and away into the forest.

The owl flew into the top of the tallest tree and perched there. The leopardess did not move. The fawn lay still.

Several moments later the doe returned.

"Speak to your fawn," said the leopardess, "and we will go."

The lamb was lying in front of the leopardess's cave, lonely, frightened, hungry, and sad. The gentle gray of dusk had become the bold black of night. She ached with emptiness. She wondered whether the leopardess and the owl would ever return. She began to think, Let me die, let me die.

Something came into the forest. The lamb did not at first know what it was, but even before she knew, her heart was soothed. She was empty but she did not ache so much. She remembered that her mother had said, "Do not be afraid. I am sure the shepherd will find you." She remembered the owl had said, "For such a young one you do well," and that the leopardess had said, "I will return as soon as I can." She ceased to think, Let me die. She stood on her shaking legs and went to see what had come into the forest.

It was the moon.

Giddy with hunger and light with emptiness, the lamb ventured out of the shadow of the cave-rock. She looked up the long slope of the hill, and there was the moon shining between the dark tree trunks, making the whole night and all The Young Woods calm with cool light.

The lamb sighed and lay down, tucking her hoofs under her, with her face to the moon. "It is not so lonely when the moon is in the forest with me," she said to herself, aloud. "The grasslands, the moon is over. The forest, the moon is in." She spoke to the moon. "I like you, Moon."

After a while the lamb saw the owl flying slantwise down the hillside. He circled over her before he spoke. "Do you see me?" he asked.

"I saw you flying down the hillside," said the lamb. "You are whiter than the moon."

The owl alighted on the ground. "Our whiteness is scarcely comparable," he said. "The moon is lucent. I am an opacity."

"But the leopardess said you were an owl!" exclaimed the lamb.

"I am an owl, also."

"There is only one of you that I can see," said the lamb, staring hard at the owl and all around him.

"Opacity is quality, not quantity," the owl said, but he saw the lamb was not listening. She was looking up the hillside.

"Something is coming," she said. "Is it death?"

"No," said the owl. "It is your milk."

The lamb rose as quickly as she could and backed toward the cave. "Milk is not like that," she said. "Oh! It is the young black leopardess. And a large thing. And a small thing."

"And milk," said the owl. He flew to the top of the tree where he had hung the third rabbit and he ate a little of it, although he was not really hungry.

The lamb backed behind the cave-rock and peered out at the leopardess and the two things following her down the moonlit hillside. As they came close the lamb went into the darkest corner of the cave and huddled there. Rustling sounds of motion neared the cave's entrance and stopped. There was a long silence before the leopardess spoke. The lamb crept a few steps out of her corner and listened.

The leopardess said, "I release you from your promise. You need not do this unless you wish to do it. If you will not give the black lamb your milk, you may go. We shall forget tonight. If you will give milk to the lamb, you and your fawn need never fear me again."

"Show me this lamb," said a light sweet voice. "I have never seen a black lamb. Until I have seen her I cannot know how I will feel about her."

The leopardess said, "Black Lamb—"

The lamb stumbled to the rear of the cave and made herself small. She could not have answered if she had wanted to: her heart had jumped into her throat and was beating there so heavily that her breath was almost stopped. The leopardess entered the cave.

"Will you come outside, Black Lamb?" she asked.

"I am afraid," gasped the lamb. "I can't help it."

"There is nothing to be afraid of," said the leopardess.

"But still I am afraid," moaned the lamb. "I can't help it!"

The leopardess picked up the lamb by the back of her neck, carried her out of the cave, and placed her in front of the doe. The lamb lay there, quivering and choking on her heart.

The doe bent her head and smelled the lamb. She walked around her, looking at her. She said, "Stand up, sweet."

The lamb stood up, but her head hung almost to the ground and she was thinking, Let me die, let me die, let me die . . .

The doe said, "Lift up your head, darling."

The lamb lifted up her head.

"Look at me, love," said the doe.

The lamb looked at the doe.

"Are you all right now?" asked the doe.

"I am all right now," replied the lamb.

"But you are hungry," said the doe.

"Yes," said the lamb, "I am hungry."

"Watch how my fawn drinks milk," said the doe. "After he has had a little, then you drink some. Will you?"

"I will," said the lamb.

3

Soon the lamb was strong enough to play with the fawn and to go with him and his mother to grassy places in the forest and, occasionally, to the grasslands. The lamb learned to watch and to be still, to look around a place before she went into it. Playing with the fawn made her hoofs and legs used to the forest.

As they grazed, the doe taught them which grasses and leaves were good to eat, which would make them well if they were ill, and which would kill them and must never be touched. One of the last was a pretty plant with clusters of green-white flowers and a subtle scent. The doe had not noticed it until the lamb said, "Look at this little flowering one!" and started to nibble a leaf to discover whether it would taste as pretty as it looked.

The doe butted the lamb in the shoulder and knocked her away from the plant. She breathed loudly before she spoke. "Do not smell it! Do not even look at it!" she whispered.

She shuddered and called her fawn. "Look once, quickly, at that flower," she whispered to him. "That is the flower I have told you about."

The fawn shivered and shrank close to his mother.

The lamb looked from the flowering plant to the doe and her fawn. They had forgotten her. With white-rimmed eyes and trembling flanks they watched the flower. The way they watched the flower made the lamb remember how she had watched the mad dog. But looking closely, yet again, at the plant, the lamb saw only the cluster of pale flowers and dark green leaves.

She heard the grass swish. The doe and her fawn were backing away, their legs awkward, their eyes furtive. The doe gave the lamb an astonished glance and said, "Come, come! Leave this place!"

The lamb followed them. They went far from there before the doe grazed again. Later the lamb asked the doe about the plant, but she said, "Never speak of it again." And she stared sternly at the lamb and turned away from her.

Since the doe had come the lamb had seldom seen the leopardess. Once she had noticed her sleeping on her willow branch and once she had caught a glimpse of her as she went, at her limping half-walk, half-run, up the hillside. The owl often talked to the doe and, unlike the leopardess, the doe always listened to what he had to say and talked to him. Neither the owl nor the doe ever mentioned the leopardess.

Now that the flower had made her shy with the doe the lamb began to miss the leopardess more. She did not see her at all that day. The next morning the doe and the fawn seemed to have forgotten the flower, and the lamb was glad, but still she missed the leopardess.

"I wonder where the young black leopardess is?" she asked the doe.

"She is not far away, Lamb," the doe replied. "She will keep her word."

"What is her word?"

"She promised to watch out for us while my fawn and I are here with you."

"Why?" the lamb asked.

"I wonder about that myself," said the doe, and as she looked at the lamb her brown eyes darkened to black. She bent her head for grass and when she had chewed and swallowed it she stepped delicately to the lamb and licked her forehead. She whispered, "Do not be afraid. I am planning to take you with us when we go."

"There is no need to whisper," said the leopardess's voice. "The lamb will go where she wishes to go."

The leopardess had been lying under some bushes. She came out where they could see her. The doe had sprung away at the first sound of her voice but after that quick movement she gazed quietly at the leopardess.

"I do not understand you, then. I think I never will," said the doe to the leopardess, "but now it is you I pity. You will break your heart if you try to break the customs of your kind. You must be a very young leopardess."

The leopardess had started away. She stopped, listened to

the doe, and turned completely around until she was facing her. "The hearts of leopards do not break," she said. "It is you who must be very young."

The doe's head jerked upward with surprise. "This is my third fawn," she said.

"May he be strong and fat as long as he lives," said the leopardess politely. She turned away and walked off among the trees.

The lamb followed her. The leopardess did not go far. She came to a fallen tree covered with thick moss and smelled it. She said, "Let us not disturb each other," and the lamb heard a high and vibrant yet shy voice say, "Yes, yes. Let us not disturb each other, black one. I have a new skin and I wish to see what is new in the forest. I am one year older this spring than last."

A dark-green snake, with green-gold and black stripes down her back and a brilliant white throat, glided from the other side of the log and coiled gracefully on the moss. She rippled her length, swayed her head in the air, and distended and deflated her white throat. Her tongue flickered in her mouth and the sunlight glinted on her black eyes.

The swaying of her head stopped as she saw the lamb. Motionless as the mossy log, she stared at her. She began to ripple and to sway again, and she said to the leopardess, "Spring is early this year."

"Yes," said the leopardess, "and you are indeed one year older this spring than last. That is a black lamb. You and she need not disturb each other. She was driven by a madness out of the grasslands and I wish her to be well and happy while she is here."

"A black lamb," repeated the snake. "It is strange, but I have never before seen a black lamb. However, I am seldom in the grasslands." She became motionless again and gazed at the lamb. "May your path be smooth and may you never disturb me," she said. She dipped her head beautifully toward the leopardess, flowed off the log, and vanished.

The leopardess made herself comfortable on the mossy log. The lamb made herself comfortable on a clump of fern.

"I think that was not death," said the lamb.

"Why not?" asked the leopardess.

"It spoke so gently to you, and it spoke gently to me too. But it is a strange thing."

"She is a snake," said the leopardess. "She is no stranger than any other thing."

"But she has no legs at all," said the lamb, "and not even two wings."

"No," said the leopardess, closing her eyes and stretching her wrists and paws, "but she goes from place to place as swiftly as she wishes."

"She begins almost the same way she ends."

"Yes," agreed the leopardess, "she does."

"Yesterday," said the lamb, "I found a small flower that made the doe and her fawn afraid. I was not afraid of it."

The leopardess raised her head from the moss. "A small flower made her afraid?" she asked. "Where is it?"

"I can remember where it is. Would you like to see it?"

"Yes," said the leopardess, and they went to see the flower.

The leopardess smelled the flower and touched it with the tip of her tongue. She bent it over and looked under it. "Perhaps the owl will know," she said.

"Perhaps what will the owl know?" the lamb asked.

"Why," said the leopardess.

They returned to the log and the fern, but the leopardess went to sleep, and so the lamb found the doe and drank milk. The leopardess was still sleeping when the lamb returned, and she settled herself on the clump of fern and waited for the leopardess to awaken. She wakened so quickly that the lamb wondered whether she had really been asleep.

"Were you asleep?" she asked.

"I was not awake," said the leopardess. "Why are you not with the doe?"

The lamb thought a moment. "I am not hungry," she said.

The leopardess's ears stood forward on her head. The lamb saw the centers of her pale eyes change from black dots of sight into dark rounds of seeing. But she said nothing, although the lamb waited for her to speak.

"Did the owl know about the flower?" asked the lamb, to keep the leopardess from going to sleep.

"He sleeps through the broad of the day. I will ask him this evening if I see him," replied the leopardess.

"The owl and the doe often talk to each other," said the lamb. "The only time you have talked to the doe was that minute this morning. I like the doe. She is sweet." The lamb paused.

"Yes," said the leopardess.

"I like you too," the lamb continued, "but I don't know why." She paused again.

But the leopardess said nothing. She looked lazily about the forest and began to wash her left foreleg. She seemed not to be listening to the lamb, but the lamb continued to talk.

"Black Leopardess," she said, "I would be happier if we were all together, you and the owl and the doe and her fawn and myself. Will you come, sometimes, and talk to the doe? Like the owl?"

"I have nothing to say to the doe," the leopardess replied, "and I am not like the owl." She got up from the moss, stretched, and sat down, her eyes fixed on the lamb.

"You talk to the owl, though. A little. Sometimes," said the lamb. She noticed as she spoke that the tip of the leopardess's tail had begun to twitch. Aside from the twitching of her tail, the leopardess was still.

"I do not eat owls," she said.

The lamb felt her heart thump once, loudly, against her ribs. "Do you eat deer?" she asked.

"Yes," said the leopardess.

"Do you eat black lambs?"

"You are the only black lamb I have ever seen," said the leopardess. "I am going now to my willow tree. The doe is over that way and down the hill a little."

The leopardess leaped off the log and went toward her willow tree. The lamb watched until she was out of sight before she returned to the doe.

"Are you all right?" asked the doe.

"I am all right," said the lamb.

4

The next morning the doe took her fawn and the lamb into the grasslands. When the sun was high they returned to the forest and found a shady hidden place for their midday rest. It happened to be the cleft where the leopardess's mother had made her home and where she had been killed, but much farther down the hillside. The cleft broadened as it went down the hill, and its banks were not so steep. The place the doe chose was at the top of a bank under the low branch of a tree which leaned over the cleft and spread itself wide to the sunlight. The small new leaves of spring hid them from sight but did not keep them from seeing.

After the doe had looked carefully about the place they made themselves comfortable for their rest. They slept a while.

Shortly after they had awakened the owl came, earlier than he had ever come before. He perched on a branch halfway up the tree and went to sleep. The doe looked about again, the lamb and the fawn ran up and down the bank, playing, and they all took another nap.

They were awakened by the leopardess. "You sleep soundly," she said.

The doe sprang up, confused, and paced here and there under the branch. "You are as quiet as the wings of night," she said. "I was not asleep. Your eyes and ears are blinding and deafening mine. Here on this hillside, with you to watch out for me, I shall soon be as helpless as a newborn fawn."

The leopardess's eyes followed every movement of the doe, but she did not speak.

"And I am getting fat," the doe continued, anger and anxiety shaking her light voice. "How far and how fast could I run today if death were behind me, or if love were before me? Ah!"

As she said "Ah!" the doe was very still and the whole of the afternoon seemed to stand still with her. She said, "Ah!" again, and the lamb and the fawn found themselves looking at four bruises on the earth where her hoofs had been. They saw the leopardess gazing up the hillside and they turned in time to see the doe vanish among distant trees near the top of the hill.

The fawn ran after his mother. He came back dancing on his hoofs and breathing fast.

"She will return, Fawn," said the owl as he floated to the low branch.

The leopardess lay with her back to the trunk of the tree. She washed her left paw. With the clean paw she washed her left ear.

They heard the doe bounding toward them from the foot of the hill. She sprang up the bank of the cleft in two leaps and stooped through the fringe of the branch. She licked the fawn and the lamb, caught her breath, and lay down, but with her head up and her feet under her.

"Am I welcome here?" the leopardess asked the doe.

The doe stared at the leopardess before she said, "This is your hillside."

The owl spoke. "The black lamb would be happier," he said in a muffled voice, "if we were all together, sometimes, and talked to one another."

The owl, the doe and her fawn, and the leopardess all fixed their eyes on the lamb.

"Oh, my," said the lamb and turned her eyes aside. But she looked into another pair of eyes. The snake was lying on a rock beside the lamb.

"Let us not disturb each other," said the snake to the lamb. "Am I welcome here?" she asked the leopardess.

"You are welcome," said the leopardess. "None of us will disturb you."

"I have cast off my old skin. I have seen the forest. There is only one new thing in the forest this spring," said the snake in her high shy voice, expanding her throat and swaying her head. Then she gazed at the lamb for a long moment of silence. "Spring is very early this year," she said at last, still staring at the lamb.

"This is the only spring I have ever seen," said the lamb. "I cannot tell whether it is early or not."

"Spring is always very early," the owl said.

There fell a silence that seemed to be endless. It was broken by the owl. He did not speak to anyone. He muttered to himself, "I wish I could cry."

"Why?" the lamb asked.

The leopardess did not give the owl time to speak. "Black Lamb," she asked, "are you one of man's animals?"

"Yes," replied the lamb. "I am the shepherd's lamb. Before I had gone out of the fold after I was born he picked me up in his arms and he said, 'This one is my own.'"

The leopardess shuddered and arched her neck. She got up and turned around and around, looking at the place where she had been lying as though it were a briar patch. She moved a little away from the tree trunk and stretched herself out again with her head on her paws. She was so still, her eyes were so pale and quiet, that the nervous jerking of her tail startled the lamb.

"What is the matter with your tail?" she asked.

The leopardess sprang straight into the air and landed, crouched and spitting, on the base of the branch under which they were sitting. Her tail lashed against the branch.

No one moved.

The lashing of the leopardess's tail became less violent, and she raised herself on the branch and turned her head stealthily to watch her tail. As she watched it, it moved more slowly, and when it was quiet, except for an occasional twitch of the tip, she jumped down from the branch and lay once more on the ground at the base of the tree.

"There is nothing the matter with my tail," she said to the lamb.

The owl made a kind of smothering sound but no one seemed to hear him. There was another long silence.

The doe said, "What is a fold, Black Lamb, where you were born and where man picked you up and said you were his own?"

"It is where we stay when lambs are born or when the snow is deep," said the lamb.

"Oh," said the doe. "Is it a thicket of evergreens or is it a cave in rock?"

"No," said the lamb. "The shepherd makes the fold out of stones and pieces of dead trees. He leads us into it and he lets us out of it."

The doe's eyes clouded as she tried to imagine this. She arose and struck at the earth with her right front hoof.

The owl made another smothering sound which caused them all to look up at him. "Calm yourself, Doe," he said. "Nothing is the matter with your tail, either."

"I— What do you mean?" asked the doe earnestly.

"I mean," said the owl, "that what you need not understand, you may as well ignore."

The doe considered this a moment; then she lay down, tucking her hoofs under her. "That is true," she said to the owl; but her eyes remained clouded and she stared at the ground without seeing it.

The owl ruffled the soft feathers of his neck and gazed thoughtfully off through the forest.

While the owl, the doe, and the lamb talked, the leopardess had seemed to go to sleep; but as soon as the owl had finished speaking she lifted her head, stretched out her crippled forearm to its full length, and yawned so broadly that her head appeared almost to split in two.

It was in the middle of this long yawn that the tiger walked under the branch and paused, his ears pricking with surprise. His pause was short. He gave a passing glance at the leopardess, a passing sniff at the lamb, and he was bending his head to seize the fawn's neck when the leopardess finished her yawn, opened her eyes, and saw him.

5

The lamb had been the first to see the tiger. His striped yellow face, with tufts of white fur at the jowls, had appeared from behind the trunk of the tree, and the lamb had time only to think, That is death, before he walked under the branch, sniffed at her, and went to the fawn.

Then things happened so quickly that the lamb had no time to think.

With a scream of rage the leopardess, who was behind the tiger, sprang through the air above and to one side of him. She flung herself around as she touched the earth and landed facing the tiger. The tiger had grunted as she passed him, and he shook his head. The leopardess had raked the side of his head with her claws. His ear was slit; there were deep scratches in his forehead; and one of the leopardess's claws had slightly torn his eyelid. A drop of blood slid into his eye and he had to lift his head from the fawn and shake the blood out to see properly.

"That fawn is mine," said the leopardess, "and this is my hillside. I wish you to go away from here."

"You will not miss this small fawn," said the tiger, with a glance at the lamb and the doe. "You have enough meat here for the whole of spring. I will take the fawn and go."

His mouth had almost closed on the fawn's neck when

the leopardess sprang into the air, landing, this time, on the tiger's back. She had again flung herself around as she sprang, and her fangs pierced the nape of the tiger's neck, her forepaws dug into his shoulders, and her hind paws cut slits down his back. The tiger coughed with surprise and pain and arched his back. The leopardess rolled off him, falling and writhing out of his reach. She crouched and faced him.

"I think you had better do your own hunting," she said, "and in some other part of the forest."

"You young black fool!" said the tiger. He threatened her with his big paw.

He turned to lick the slits in his back, and the leopardess, a dark streak of speed, raked the side of his throat and his cheek with the long claws of her crippled paw and was out of his reach again.

The tiger turned from the fawn and gave all his attention to the leopardess. "Very well, black one," he said. "I had no wish to harm you, but you leopards always were too small for your brains."

The instant the tiger turned, the doe nudged the fawn and the lamb to their feet and hurried them away from the tree. They were all shaking with fear, the doe as much as the fawn and the lamb, but the doe murmured calmly to the two little ones, "Quickly, quickly, run, run. The faster we run, the less we will fear. We are safe now, but we must find a hidden place as soon as we can."

"What will happen to the young leopardess?" asked the lamb.

"Oh, run, run!" exclaimed the doe. "This is no time for questions!" She bumped and shoved the lamb to push her onward, but the lamb braced her little black hoofs and would not be pushed.

"What will happen to the leopardess?" she repeated.

The doe curveted with impatience. "She is well able to take care of herself," she said, "and as soon as we are safely away, that is what she will do."

"But that is death, and large, and she is only a young black leopardess, and small," said the lamb. "You and the fawn go. I have to stay here. I can't help it."

"Do as the doe tells you," said the owl, "and don't stand there saying, 'I can't help it.' It is you who will be the death of the leopardess, not the tiger."

"How could I—" the lamb began, but the owl said to the doe, "Take your fawn and go. The leopardess would wish you to. I will do what I can for this strange mad creature."

The doe and her fawn went. The owl flew down beside the lamb. With his head cocked toward the sounds the leopardess and the tiger were making he walked up and down and talked rapidly.

"We will go now, as fast as you can, to the leopardess's lair. I will go with you." He flew off the ground and hovered above the lamb. The lamb did not move, and so he alighted beside her and talked again. "Before long the leopardess will go to her cave. She will expect you to be waiting for her there."

"I will wait here," said the lamb.

The owl stopped and stiffened. Every one of his feathers ruffled out, so that he seemed to swell to twice his size. His eyes bulged. A hissing sound came through his closed beak. Suddenly his feathers fell into place. "This is out of my sphere," he said. "Farewell, Black Lamb." He flew off through the forest.

The lamb went to the tree. She could tell by the sounds they were making that the leopardess and the tiger were coming toward it, and so she stayed there. She was weak with fear and had to lean against the trunk of the tree to keep from falling.

A voice spoke.

Her heart had nearly burst with fright before she recognized it. It was the owl's voice.

"Do you see me?" he asked.

"I see you," whispered the lamb. "I am glad you came back."

"I am not glad," said the owl, "but I am here. Keep the tree trunk between yourself and the—"

Before the owl could finish his warning the leopardess bounded up the bank and sprang to the low branch. She was panting, but her eyes blazed with triumph.

"I will have one more word with him," she said to the owl, "and then I will let this striped thief alone with his bad temper. He is quick for his size, but he is not so quick as I am."

The leopardess licked a gash in her shoulder and lowered her head to the branch. She had stretched limply along it to rest while she could. Down in the cleft below the bank the tiger could be heard telling the leopardess what he would do to her when he caught her. The leopardess had led him between two tall steep rocks in the bottom of the cleft, where he had, for a while, stuck.

The lamb came from behind the tree.

"I am sorry to shorten your rest," said the owl, "but look below you. The black lamb stayed here because death is large and you are only a young black leopardess, and small. The doe and her fawn are safe by now. I think the lamb is tired of milk and wishes to taste death."

"The doe ran off and left her?" asked the leopardess without moving or opening her eyes.

"Oh, no!" said the lamb. "She tried to make me go with her and the owl tried to take me away too. But I could not leave you here alone with death."

The leopardess looked down at the lamb. "That is not death," she said. "That is a tiger. Will you stay behind the tree until the owl or I tell you to go?"

The lamb went behind the tree.

The leopardess looked at everything she could see as the tiger came over the edge of the bank. He was shaking the blood out of his eyes; the leopardess had scratched the other eyelid. The owl heard the leopardess say, softly, "Hah!" as though she had discovered something. Then she flattened herself along the branch and watched the tiger.

The tiger was frantic with rage and humiliation and he was burning with the lust to kill, not only the leopardess but

anything that lived. His mouth hung open and his breath
twanged in his throat. He saw the owl first and raised his
heavy length and stretched out his great paw with a swift-
ness remarkable for his size. The owl flew over the tiger's
back to distract his attention from the leopardess.

"Tiger," said the owl, "I advise you to leave this hillside
while you can see to walk. If leopards are too small for their
brains, then tigers would certainly seem to be too large for
theirs."

"Owls are nearly all eyes and feathers," said the leopardess, "and the little meat on their bones is very tough." She
had sat up on the branch and was licking the silky fur on
her chest. "Have you ever eaten mice, Tiger? They are small,
harmless, and easy to catch if you are quick enough. I know
a little wildcat who would be glad to teach you."

Moaning with the pain of his hatred, the tiger turned
from the owl and sprang toward the leopardess. Just in time
to escape his claws she leaped over his head. The owl flew
to the branch.

The fight lasted only a short time, but it was violent and
terrible. The owl did not once close his eyes and yet he did
not see it all. The hotly powerful lunges of the tiger, the
cold precision of the leopardess's attacks and escapes, were
too swift even for the large eyes of an old owl.

The owl could not understand after the fight had begun
why the leopardess did not leave the branch and carry the
fight to the hillside or into the cleft. She stayed on the
branch or under it or near it all during the fight. Once for
the instant she was beside him on the branch the owl spoke

anxiously. "Why must you stay here? Lead him away and lose him. I will take the lamb to your lair."

The leopardess did not have time to answer and if she had had time she could not have spared the breath. The owl heard the sob of her desperate breathing as she backed away along the branch from the thrusts of the tiger's paw. Leaping above his paw she ran along the branch and dived over the tiger's head.

The owl dug his talons into the branch and stretched his wings out from his sides. "Ah," he whispered. "A-ah! A-a-a-a-h!" The tiger seemed to have caught the leopardess before she could recover from her long leap. But she twisted, rolled, threw herself backward, and escaped yet again.

Soon after this the owl heard a cobweb of sound weaving through the thick rough sounds of the fight. Then he saw the snake and then he knew why the leopardess was staying under the branch.

And she did do what she had planned. With her final surge of strength the leopardess succeeded in leading the tiger so that he stepped on the snake.

The snake had been lying on the ground, close along the rock beside which the lamb had lain. As the tiger felt the snake he lifted his paw and seemed to freeze. The leopardess also froze where she crouched.

"I was hoping you would not disturb me," said the snake, and now her diffident, wavering voice could be plainly heard. As she spoke, her long green length was coiling itself with a speed and intricacy that made the tiger dizzy. Then the snake was coiled. "I warned you, but you would not hear me," she said. And still the tiger did not move. Nothing moved.

"Begone!" said the snake. She hurled her flat head, struck the tiger in the shoulder, and was coiled again. But she did not have to strike twice.

The tiger staggered out from the branch, his eyes glazed with terror, and stumbled into the cleft. But the leopardess leaped to the edge of the bank and said, "Tiger, go down to the river. You will find the spiny-leaf growing there." The tiger stopped to listen, and then he could be heard crashing toward the river and the plant that might save his life.

The leopardess lay on the ground and closed her eyes. Her flat sides heaved with her exhausted breathing, but the owl heard her whispering, "This—is my—hillside—and I—am—large enough—for my brain."

6

The doe had hidden her fawn in the nearest safe place she remembered. She ran back to the cleft to do what she could to help the leopardess. She might be able to distract the tiger's attention from her and lead him away. She could keep out of his reach, she knew, as long as he was unable to surprise her. She stood with the lamb behind the tree and heard the last of the fight.

As soon as it was over she brought her fawn back, and soon after the doe and her fawn had returned, the leopardess opened her eyes and gave herself a thorough washing with her tongue. She stretched, gave a few extra licks to the gash in her shoulder, which had almost stopped bleeding; and then she looked with wide eyes at the owl, the doe and her fawn, and the lamb, as though she was surprised to see them.

She thought a moment. She returned to the place where she had been lying when the tiger appeared and she re-arranged herself exactly as she had been at that instant. They all returned to their places.

The lamb sensed a movement beside her and saw the snake glide on the rock. The snake and the leopardess made each other a little bow. The snake draped her length there and swayed her head and flickered her tongue. Then she said shyly, "It was man and his fold we were talking about. I have never seen man or a fold."

"Man is not new in the forest this spring," said the owl, "or out of the forest, either. I have seen man. I think man would disturb you."

"Young Black Leopardess," said the doe in a grave gentle voice, "you have kept your word twice over. You have snatched my fawn from the opened jaws of the tiger. Let us be friends forever, you and I."

The leopardess glanced at the doe. She got up and limped down the hillside, but she stopped a short way off and with her back to them all stood so still that not even the tip of her tail twitched. She turned slowly. "No," she said to the doe, but she did not look at her as she spoke. "No, we can-not be friends."

"No," said the doe, gazing off through the trees as she spoke. "That is true. We cannot be friends."

The leopardess turned away again. She licked the gash in her shoulder as though she were angry with it. She limped a few more steps beyond the branch, almost as the tiger had staggered away after the snake had struck him.

The owl sidled up and down the branch, hissing to himself. The fawn looked at his mother, saw wetness in her eyes, and his own eyes were wet. The lamb felt a hot pain come into her heart. She thought, What is this that is coming into my heart? Is it death? The snake's tongue flickered, her eyes glinted, and her head swayed as she tried to see all of them at once.

The leopardess faced the doe again and came almost to the edge of the branch. She held her crippled paw against her chest as she spoke, and her eyes were very wide. Her voice shook. "But we are not enemies, you and I," she said. "We never were enemies—"

"No," said the doe gently, in the same voice she used when she spoke to her fawn to calm him. "No, we never were enemies, black one. We never will be enemies."

From deep in the leopardess's throat there came an odd blurred snarl. She frisked like a kitten, batting with her paw at a fern frond and biting at it fiercely. She ran in a circle after her tail. She stopped to lick her shoulder as though she had forgotten her tail; and then, suddenly pouncing on her tail, she gave it two or three licks.

She looked all around her. A large black and yellow butterfly was fluttering up the hillside and, with another blur of sound, the leopardess scampered away from the branch and pursued the butterfly. She leaped high in the air and crouched low on the ground and she dashed slant-wise, on the tips of her paws, with her back arched. When she went out of sight among the trees she had not yet caught the butterfly.

"Oh, my," exclaimed the lamb after the leopardess was out of sight, "what is the matter with the young black leopardess?"

"Youth," said the owl. "But that is a fever from which most of us recover."

"No," said the doe, "it comes and goes in us as long as we live, like spring. But you are older than I am, Owl. Is that true?"

"That is true," said the owl and flew away.

PART THREE

I

Several days after the leopardess's fight with the tiger, the owl decided to take his midday rest near the doe so that they could talk between naps. It was warm for spring, and he had to search far and wide before he saw the cool thicket the doe had chosen. But as soon as he found the doe she asked him where she could find the leopardess. The owl had seen her near her willow tree, and the doe and her fawn and the lamb went there.

The owl was curious to know why the doe wanted to see the leopardess. He followed her, swinging drowsily on his wings. He nearly bumped into a very busy thrush, and the remarks the thrush made about his flying wakened him thoroughly. He flew fast to his perch in the leopardess's willow, and as he awaited the arrival of the doe he remembered with irritation and respect what the thrush had said about him. "Hyperbole," he muttered, "but on a twig of truth."

The leopardess was asleep on her branch. She pricked her ears before the doe came in sight, but she did not lift her head until the three were standing near the branch.

"I wish to talk with you about the black lamb," said the doe. "Shall we talk before we sleep, or afterward?"

"Perhaps we could talk better after we have slept," the leopardess suggested.

"Oh, my," said the lamb. "What now?"

"Nothing that can interfere with our sleep," said the doe.

"I am not sleepy," said the lamb.

"Perhaps we could sleep better after we have talked," suggested the leopardess.

"Yes," said the owl, and the doe glanced at the lamb and said, "Yes" too.

The leopardess leaped from the willow branch.

"In a little while," said the doe, "the lamb will not need milk, and I have already been absent too long from my own groves. You said the lamb would go where she wishes to go?"

"Yes," said the leopardess.

The doe turned to the lamb. "Will you wish to go with me, Black Lamb, or will you stay here with the young black leopardess and the white owl?" The lamb did not answer, and the doe continued, "I will be happy if you come with me, and I think my herd will be happy to have you."

"Will the leopardess and the owl go with us?" the lamb asked, but she knew they would not. No one spoke. The lamb's head began to spin, and her heart ached. She did not know where she wished to go.

After they had waited a while the doe and the fawn lay down and the leopardess leaped to her willow branch. When next the lamb noticed them they were asleep; but the owl was awake. He saw the lamb look at him. He spread out his wings and glided down beside her.

"The possibilities are infinite but the probabilities are few and as follows—" he began, then stopped. He went close to the lamb and whispered, "Temporize."

"What?" whispered the lamb.

"You have never lived with the doe's herd—"

"No."

"Or in her groves?"

"No."

The owl glanced toward the leopardess and pressed his little hooked beak closer to the lamb's ear. "Until you have lived with the doe's herd and in her groves how can you tell whether you would rather go with the doe or stay here with—us?"

"Oh," whispered the lamb.

"Well?" whispered the owl.

"It is hard for me to tell," whispered the lamb. "But why are we whispering?" she said aloud.

"Yes, why?" asked the leopardess. The doe and the fawn lifted their heads. The owl flew to the top of the willow tree.

"The black lamb does not know your groves or your herd," said the leopardess to the doe, "nor does your herd know her. Could she be with you a while before she makes up her mind?"

"That is what I have been thinking should be done," said the doe.

They started that evening. The owl flew ahead, the leopardess was a little behind him, the fawn and the lamb trotted behind the leopardess, and last came the doe. They traveled all night and the early part of the next morning, resting when the fawn and the lamb were tired. The warm clouds of the day became a steady drizzle of cold rain at night. They went up, down, and around hills; across and along brooks; through rocky fields, low thickets of scrub brush, and low and high and thick and thin forest growth. They saw the misty shapes and heard the small sounds of a few animals and night-flying birds; but nothing bothered them, although they were far from the safety of the leopardess's hillside.

In the gray light of the rainy morning, on the brink of a small lake in a deep valley, the leopardess turned back.

"The owl will go with you until you have found the deer," she said to the doe. "I think you will find them soon, and I will leave you here because I do not want to scatter the herd. The owl will visit you and bring me word of the black lamb. I wish you well, Doe."

"I wish you well forever, black one," said the doe.

The lamb said, "Are you going to your hillside now, Black Leopardess?"

"Yes," said the leopardess.

"When will I see you again?" the lamb asked.

"I do not know," the leopardess replied. "I will not hunt in the groves of the doe's herd, while her herd is in them."

She looked at the doe. "I will never hunt in your groves while you graze there unless I have to, and do not forget that you and your fawn are welcome and safe in my edge of the forest even if I should be starving."

"I will never forget," said the doe.

"And am I welcome too, Black Leopardess?" asked the lamb. "And do you wish me well?"

"Yes," said the leopardess.

Something burned in the lamb's eyes, and she closed them. When she opened her eyes the leopardess was gone.

The doe licked the lamb's forehead. "Come along, Lamb."

"Something is tight in my throat," said the lamb. "It hurts."

The owl alighted on the ground and cocked his head solemnly to one side. "Nothing is the matter with your throat," he said, "but something is the matter with your head. You are having delusions of duality. You cannot be a deer and a cat. You have to be a black lamb." The owl cocked his head to the other side, blinked his eyes rapidly, and stared hard at the lamb. "Whatever that is," he added. "Are you all right now?" he asked.

"Owl," said the lamb, "you talk too much."

"You are all right," said the owl. "Shall we proceed?" he asked the doe, and they went slowly on along the shore of the lake.

They went around the lake, crossed a stream that flowed out of it, and began to climb a steep hill. If the hill had been steeper it would have been a cliff, and the fawn and the lamb were glad when they came to the top of it and saw before them a level floor of the forest. These trees were not tall, but their trunks were thick and gnarled. Their leaves, even early in spring, were large and so greedy for sunlight that few bushes and little grass grew beneath them. Because of the mistiness of the morning, the depth of the forest, and the sheer drop to the curved valley behind them, it seemed to be a forest on a cloud.

The fawn and the lamb stopped to catch their breath, but the doe ran lightly into the forest. The owl perched above the fawn and the lamb.

When the doe returned through the foglike rain between the damp trees her hoofs seemed hardly to touch the wet leaves on the ground. "Follow me," she said, "as quietly as you can." She had forgotten the owl. He made a small sound to remind her he was there. She looked at him. "White one," she said, "my herd is near this forest. You have flown far with us, and now we are safe. In a few days the black lamb will be able to tell you where she will make her home. I wish you well forever, Owl."

The owl's eyes grew larger and rounder but he merely said, "I will see you here and there and when the lamb seems to know what she wants we will talk together. Meanwhile I wish you well, and your fawn. And you, Black Lamb, I am your friend as long as you need me."

The lamb's throat hurt again. "If I don't need you, you won't be my friend?" she asked.

"Ah, me," said the owl, "you are having that trouble with your head again! I will be your friend whether you need me or not. Now is your head all right?"

"It is my throat, Owl," said the lamb. "Something gets tight in it."

"The doe is impatient to find her—her herd," said the owl. "A remarkably foggy morning, isn't it?" He swooped out of sight among the treetops.

The doe seemed unaware he had gone. "Come," she said, and darted into the mists, only to dart back again and urge them to be quick and quiet.

The fawn danced excitedly on his hoofs, like his mother, but the lamb was too puzzled to dance. She followed them. She looked from side to side, at the strange trees, through the wet air, and she watched with astonished eyes the antics of the doe and the fawn.

The fog thinned and the morning grew brighter.

The doe returned from one of her disappearances in the mists and said in a whisper, "Slowly, now. Here is some grass. We will eat a little of it as we go. But slowly, slowly."

The lamb looked for grass and found a few bitter blades. She was more astonished than ever when, as she started to ask "What grass?" she saw the doe. The doe was grazing so slowly, she might have been up to her shoulders in the heaviest of sweet grasses. The fawn seemed astonished too, but he did the best he could to imitate his mother.

"What grass are you eating?" the lamb asked.

"Eat," whispered the doe, "and be quiet!" She stepped forward with her head still lowered.

The lamb looked more carefully for grass and found no grass. They had passed the poor small patch and all the lamb could see were some plants she had tasted and knew were sour, and dead leaves. The lamb was worrying about her eyes when she heard the leaves rustle and a gasping sigh. She looked, and there was a buck glaring at them, the thin mist wreathing his antlers.

The doe and the fawn gave no sign they had seen or heard the buck. They went on eating the invisible grass.

The lamb did not know how to eat invisible grass and so she watched to see what would happen. She was not afraid, because the doe had been telling her about deer, how some were bucks and had antlers and some were does and had fawns.

This was a buck, but prongs were broken off his antlers. He was thin and there were scars on his hide. The lamb thought he must never have seen a doe, because he trembled as though he were frightened. The lamb felt she should say to him, "That is not death, that is a doe," but the doe had told her to be quiet.

The doe grazed closer to the buck and it was only as she seemed about to touch him that she looked up. She sprang away from the buck and said, "Oh, sweet! How you frightened me!"

The buck closed his eyes and, sighing, he approached the doe. He licked her face, rubbed his neck against hers, and all the time he was moaning, "Sweet— Oh, my darling— Oh, my love!" and large tears rolled out of his eyes and fell on the doe or on the ground. The doe drooped her head sadly too, but the lamb noticed that no tears fell from her eyes.

After the buck had somewhat recovered the doe stepped

back from him. "Why, what has happened to you?" she
cried. "Your broken antlers—your poor sharp bones—your
scarred hide! Come, little ones, follow us."

As they went through the forest the buck told the doe how
he had searched for her through the groves and over the
grasslands, and the doe told him about the black lamb, the
young black leopardess, the white owl, the snake, and the
tiger. The buck hurriedly licked the lamb's forehead, said,
"You are welcome, little one," and returned to the side of
the doe.

"I suppose the herd will be in the round place?" asked
the doe. "Or have we not yet left the high place?"

"Ah, what does it matter where the herd is?" said the
buck. "I have found my love again."

The doe walked closer to the buck and whispered, "Do
you think they will be happy to have the little black one?"

"Ah!" sighed the buck, "What did you say?"

"Come, little ones," said the doe. To the buck she said,
"I was asking if you are happy now?"

The buck sighed again.

2

Soon the mist melted and the sun shone on a shining world.
The gnarled old trees seemed young. The fresh green of
their leaves spread over canopies of smooth light brown
twigs and the heavy bark of the thick trunks was soft with
dampness. Even the dead leaves, brown on the brown earth,
spread through the lower air a rich and living fragrance.

The fawn and the lamb played. They ran after each other in wide curves and sharp angles of delight. They sprang into the warm air, all their hoofs off the ground at once. They made long leaps and quick stops, and tossed and lowered their heads, and soft shapeless sounds bubbled in the backs of their throats.

Before they knew where they were they had dashed out of the forest and into a round expanse of grassy land. The grass was bright green and its scent in the wider air was as keen as its color. The fawn and the lamb stared at the bright green and breathed its free-flowing sweetness. Then they ran twice as fast, leaped twice as high; and the tossings of their heads, their turns and capers, were as light as the flight of swallows in dusk, as swift as the playing of minnows in a clear stream.

They stopped for breath. They leaned against each other with hanging heads. "Oh, my," said the lamb.

Out of the groves and across the grass came many deer— bucks and does and fawns. One by one, waiting their turns as they approached, they looked at the fawn and the lamb, especially at the lamb. They stooped their proud heads to smell them, and several of the does licked the lamb's forehead. The fawns stayed behind but cast friendly glances at the lamb.

The lamb felt shy, but she was not afraid. She knew her own doe and buck were standing behind them, murmuring to each other of love, but soon the doe sprang forward. She said, "Lift up your heads, little ones," and remained until all the deer had looked at them and wandered off to graze

among the hillocks of grass or into the groves around the
grassy place.

Last of all came a very old doe. She walked as lightly as
the others, but slowly. Her brown hide was sprinkled with
white hairs which shone silver in the sun, and she was thin.
Her eyes were dark and deep. The fawn and the lamb could
not help lowering their heads as she looked at them.

"Little ones," said the young doe, "this is my very-great
grandmother. She is the old one of the herd." And she began to explain to the old doe about the lamb.

"Yes, yes," said the old one, "I have already been told
the story of the black lamb several times. Be quiet, child,
while I look at her." She said, "Look at me, Lamb," and the
lamb looked into her eyes.

The old doe licked the lamb's forehead. "You are hungry, sweet," she said.

"Yes," said the lamb. "We have walked all night."

"Come with me a while," said the old one.

The young doe said, "Yes, Lamb. Always do what the
old one of the herd tells you to do. She is wise and good.
She will take care of you."

The lamb gazed again at the old one and her heart felt
as quiet as the doe's deep eyes. "You will take care of me,"
she said.

"As long as I can," said the old one, and they walked together across the round place. The deer lowered their heads
to the old one as she passed and they looked kindly at the
lamb. The lamb could not help skipping a little as she
walked beside the old doe. She was happy.

They went into a spacious grove of tall trees with high tops. Clumps of bushes grew among them, casting a darker shade over the pale shade of the treetops. After a long walk through these trees the lamb heard the exquisite sound of water falling through a height of air into a depth of water. It was a small but clear spring and its water fell into a small but deep pool. The old doe drank first. The lamb had never tasted water so fresh and cool. They went on. It was quiet; no other deer were grazing in that grove.

The stream broadened in a level place into a wide pool, and around the pool the ground was covered with little green-white flowers and the air was full of their subtle scent. The lamb looked closely at the plants. Yes, the leaves of the plant were dark green with light green veins and the stems were thick and moist.

The old doe had stopped in the middle of a patch of the flowers. She said, "Taste these flowers, Black Lamb."

The lamb gazed at her fearfully. Are you death? she thought. She remembered well that the young doe had told her never to touch this plant when they had seen it in the edge of the forest. But the doe had also said the old one would take care of her.

The lamb ate two or three sprays of the flower, and then she told the old one how frightened the young doe had been when they had seen this plant on the leopardess's hillside.

The old one grazed on the flowers in silence for several moments. "These flowers are only for the old ones of the herd," she said, "very old ones who have lived many years and seen much of the earth and learned how life comes and goes." She tossed her head and curveted so lightly and beautifully that she seemed to fly. "Now you have tasted this plant," she said. "Do you like it?"

"I do like it," said the lamb. "It is better—it is better than milk. But I am only a black lamb. I cannot even tell whether spring is early this year, or late. I do not think I have learned well how life comes and goes."

The old doe licked the lamb's forehead. "You have learned many things, Lamb," she said. "Now eat as much of this flower as you wish. It is indeed better than milk."

They grazed on the green-white flowers all the rest of the morning, and when they were tired they found a fresh patch of the flowers and took their naps in the middle of it. The lamb was so happy that she slept sweetly.

3

The old doe awakened the lamb late in the afternoon and after they had eaten the flowers and drunk from the deep spring they started to the grassy place. The lamb ran and leaped and danced around the old one as they went.

"Little black one—" said the old doe, lifting her head high. The lamb ran to her. "Be quiet a moment." The lamb heard nothing but the old one said, "Now we must hurry. I think we will be there in time. They are coming from the opposite side of the round place."

"What is coming?" the lamb asked.

"Hurry," said the old one. "Keep close beside me."

As they ran the lamb heard sounds that made her heart lonely with remembered fear. The sounds were distant, but she could hear them plainly enough to know that they were the sounds not of one but of many dogs. Their barking and growling frayed the air and tangled it with knotted noise. The breeze was blowing the other way, and she could not smell them, but the stench of the mad dog who had driven her and her mother into The Young Woods came back from her memory and fouled her throat.

No other deer had been grazing near the flowery place, but as they neared the grassy place they were passed by bucks or does with fawns. These paid no attention to the old doe and the lamb, except one stalwart young buck galloping headlong through the trees. He braced himself to a grinding stop and pranced behind them.

But the old doe said, "Are you a motherless fawn? Go where you belong! I am still able to guard this little one and my own old self as well as I once guarded you. Go, child!"

The young buck lowered his head to her and ran on. The old doe said proudly, "That was one of my very-great grandsons," but the lamb was too frightened to speak. They were near the end of the grove and the sounds of the dogs were mingled with other sounds—heavy snorts of breath, thuds and dull crackings of bone, the trampling of many hoofs, and sometimes a shrill yelp or a strangled gasp of agony.

At the edge of the grove the old doe ran first into the midst of a thicket and stopped to look into the grassy place; and the lamb, frightened as she was, looked through the leaves too. The sight she saw increased her fear but all the loneliness left her heart.

She saw in the center of the round place a moving and shifting circle of bucks surrounding an inner circle of does, and, in the center, all the fawns of the herd.

The noise came from the opposite side of the circles and the lamb saw no dogs until a buck ran out with two dogs hanging at his throat and two more snapping and jumping at his flanks. The buck shook off one of the dogs at his throat and trampled him with his front hoofs, but as he did this the dogs behind him seized and tore his legs and brought him to the ground. The three dogs killed the buck and ran back out of sight behind the circle.

Then the circle began to turn, slowly, in the direction of the old doe and the lamb, and as it turned, small groups of dogs came into sight.

The old doe said, "Quickly, Lamb. Run as fast as you can and I will run beside you," and she broke through the bushes, waited until the lamb was beside her, and they began their run toward the circles of deer.

They were halfway across the open space before a dog saw them. He detached himself from a group of five or six dogs trying to cut a yearling buck out of his place in the circle and came toward them, his teeth white in a grin of hungry pleasure.

The lamb panted to the old one, "Look! Look!" but the doe ran on as before and the lamb had no more strength for speech, but she thought, The old one does not see it. Now we will die.

But the old doe had seen the dog, although she pretended not. She waited until the dog was making his last rush toward the lamb. She seemed to see the dog, to be afraid and leap ahead of the lamb, to one side of the dog, and at the top of his last lunge her sharp hind hoofs dealt the dog a crashing crushing blow on the shoulder and the side of the head.

The lamb stopped. She was too breathless and too terrified to run another step. She hung her head and gasped, "Let me die, let me die, let me die—"

The old doe pushed her and said, "Run, Lamb, run. Never stop running."

The lamb tried to run but she saw dogs leave the circle and start toward them, and although they were now close to the deer the lamb could see that, fast as she might run, the dogs would reach her before she could reach the deer. She panted, "Leave me, Old One. I cannot run fast enough."

But the old one stood beside the lamb and called in her high old voice, "We have run our distance! Can you help us?"

Before she called, the circle of deer had bulged toward them, and even before that the lamb had seen the buck with the broken antlers hurl himself out of his place in the circle toward the approaching dogs. With wide white rims around his black eyes, with red, distended nostrils, he lowered his antlers and plunged into the midst of the dogs. The last thing the lamb saw as the circles closed around her was the young doe herself, plunging out behind her buck, white-eyed and screaming, "That is my lamb!" and terrifying the dogs with the terrible dancing of her hoofs.

The old doe saw that the lamb was safe in the crowd of fawns before she took her place in the circle of does.

The lamb was shivering. Her bones seemed to be rattling, but she was not afraid, and she thought as she shivered, I will never be afraid again. She felt a gentle touch on her forehead and saw the young doe's fawn licking her face and saying, "My sister, are you all right now?" and surprise stopped her shivering. As many days as she had eaten and played and slept with him and his mother, those were the first words she had heard him speak.

"I am all right now," the lamb said, and before she realized what she was doing she had licked the fawn's forehead and said, "Sweet."

Together they moved through the crowd of fawns until they could see the young doe and the buck with the broken antlers. They were safely in their places in the circles, and the harshest sounds of the battle had shifted away from them.

Before long these sounds grew fewer and fainter. There were only enough dogs running around the circles of deer to hold them there while the rest of the pack escaped. All at once the circle of bucks broke and they ran into the surrounding groves in pursuit of the last of the dogs. Then the does left their circle and each ran to her fawn and calmed and comforted it.

But several bucks and a doe had been killed and others were badly hurt. The young doe's flank was torn and she limped a little. The grass was trampled flat and stained with blood, and the smell of blood stained the clear air. Nevertheless, the deer were pleased. They said to one another, "The wild dogs will not return here next spring," and glanced at the dead bodies of the dogs. When all the bucks had returned they told of overtaking and killing more of the dogs, and the deer said, "They will not return here for two or three springs."

The old doe told the lamb that the deer and the wild dogs fought each other in the round place often, that sometimes the dogs were scattered and sometimes the deer. The lamb asked why the deer did not stay away from the round place and she replied, "This is our place. This early grass is full of strength. These groves are high and pleasant. The herd is glad to spill its blood for this place."

"But the blood and the smell of the blood, and the dead deer and dogs—" said the lamb. "How could you ever eat this grass again?"

"The place will soon be cleansed of death," said the old doe, "and next spring there will be new grass. Look above you."

The lamb looked into the sky and saw many black birds circling there, and she understood that as soon as the herd left the place the birds would drop into it and eat the flesh off the bones of the dead deer and dogs.

Already the deer were preparing to leave. The wounded bucks were dragging themselves into a thicket of thorn trees, where they would hide until they were strong enough to find the herd or until they died. Their does and fawns stared after them but did not follow: they knew they must stay with the herd. The lamb saw a doe lick the forehead of a dead buck and then run into the forest, followed by her fawn.

The buck with the broken antlers ran to the young doe. He licked her forehead and the hide around the torn place in her flank before he followed the rest of the bucks to look for danger along the way the herd was going.

The old doe said, "Come, Lamb. Now we are going down into the singing valley. It is not far." The two does turned toward the eastern grove, and the fawn and the lamb followed them.

4

It was as the herd went down through woods and clearings in a long straggling line that the lamb began to think, sadly, that she could not live with the deer. For one thing, her legs were too short, she could hardly keep up with them, and her shorter legs had given the wild dogs their chance to kill the old doe and herself. The old one alone could have reached the circle of deer quite safely.

For another thing, the deer were too sudden as well as too swift. They would graze in one place as they went toward the singing valley and, before the lamb could enjoy the grass, off they would go to another clump of shrubs or small clearing. And by the time the lamb had caught up with them and looked around, the deer had eaten all they wanted there and were disappearing in another direction.

The old and the young doe and often the buck with the broken antlers guarded the lagging lamb all the way. Even so, she was too tired to graze happily in the singing valley after she reached it. She found a quiet place as soon as she arrived there and said she would rest while the others grazed as they wished.

As she rested and listened to the singing of the valley she felt better. The valley sang with the sound of water falling and flowing. On three sides the place was surrounded by steep terraced hills or cliffs of rock, and down all these heights, from the three sides, fell streams of water of all sizes, from a tiny trickle of drops to a tall steaming column of white foam. And yet, in spite of the hundreds of watery voices, the valley was peaceful. It was broad and very green, with a thousand tints and shades of green. The moist air was stirred by ten thousand ripples and currents of wet wind.

One part of the valley was a marsh, but through the rest of it, in a net of streams, grew many grasses, bushes, small trees; and below the center and most sloping cliff was a grove of giant trees. The deer had descended into the valley down the slope above the grove, and the small shelf of grassy terrace where the lamb was resting was to one side of it. She could see most of the valley.

She watched the deer scatter through its breadth and length. The herd spread through the wide watery place, some leaping over the streams, some grazing along the banks. They were never still. As some ate slowly in deep grass, others roamed from grass to bush to tree, snatching their bites as they went.

The lamb nibbled at the grass she could reach and wished the young doe were near, so she could drink milk. She had just put down her head for a nap when the doe bounded to her, followed by the fawn, and said, "Lamb, you must drink milk. Are you all right?"

"I am all right," said the lamb. She drank milk. "Will we stay long in this valley?" she asked.

"Tonight and tomorrow and tomorrow night," said the doe, "and then early the next morning we must go to another place."

"Why?" asked the lamb. "This is a large valley, full of grasses. Why must you leave it so soon?"

"We never stay long here," said the doe.

"Why not?" the lamb persisted. "Will death come?"

The doe seemed puzzled. "We have never had to fight here. I do not know why we stay only a few days." She looked out over the valley.

Darkness and a gray mist were rising. The final rays of the sun struck the rim of the cliffs above them and the lamb could hear through the sounds of the falling waters the evening songs of strange birds. The old doe came toward them along the grassy terrace from the grove of giant trees, and the lamb asked her why they did not stay longer in the singing valley.

Before she replied to the lamb's question the old one turned her head, as the young doe had done, and gazed out over the valley.

"I do not remember it myself," she said, "but when I was a

fawn the old one of the herd told me that the grass was poor that year in other places and so the herd stayed here a long time. Then a sickness came upon us. Many laid themselves down and slept, and they never wakened. I think this valley belongs to a herd of waters. The waters do not mind if we stay a short time but—"

The old doe paused and licked the lamb's forehead. "You can see it yourself, Lamb. This valley belongs to a herd of waters, and it is theirs, not ours," she continued. "Now let us find some grass that is full of strength, because this has been a hard day. We must sleep well."

As they went deeper into the valley the young doe said to her fawn, "Did you hear what the old one told us? Always remember it, Fawn. Some time you may be the old one of the herd and so every day you must learn to be wise and good."

"I will always remember," said the fawn. "I will learn every day," and he looked shyly at the old one.

The old doe rubbed her face against his and butted him playfully in the shoulder. "And you must be strong as well as wise," she said to him, "and quick as well as good. To be an old one in The Young Woods you must have sharp antlers and brave legs as well as sharp eyes and ears and a brave heart. Always remember that too, Very-Great Grandson."

"I never will forget it, Old One," said the fawn and he tossed his head as though the antlers were already there and gazed sternly into the singing valley.

The lamb noticed that the old one and the young doe glanced at each other over the fawn's head and lifted their own heads proudly.

The next day the lamb found delectable grasses, and the water of every stream had its own delicious flavor. The old doe stayed with the lamb and, while they grazed, told of the pleasant or sorrowful things that had happened to her or to the herd. The young doe and the fawn were with them during the midday rest. They listened to the singing of the waters and slept deeply; but even in their sleep the voices of the waters spoke to them, and they could hardly tell when they slept and when they were awake.

In the afternoon the young doe and her fawn went to other parts of the valley. The old one and the lamb grazed near their resting place. The brook there contained sweet water which felt soft in the mouth. The grass too was softly sweet and seemed to have no substance, only flavor. The water did not quench their thirst and they drank a great deal of it, especially the old doe. The lamb neither drank nor ate so much because she had drunk milk before the young doe left them.

The sun had descended only halfway to darkness when the doe said, "I think I will rest in the shade of those bushes. My old bones need more sleep than yours. Stay here if you wish. Nothing will harm you in this valley. But you can soon find the young doe if you would rather graze with her."

"I will stay with you," said the lamb.

The lamb grazed alone. She came upon another kind of grass with a sharper taste and grazed toward the brook for a drink. She went to speak to the old one, but she was asleep.

Later the lamb also became sleepy and decided to rest near the old doe. She was surprised to find her still sound asleep, in the same place, in the same position.

She is tired with all her years, the lamb thought as she looked at the thin silver-brown body of the old one. How many days and nights of forest and grassland she has seen! How many hills and valleys her hoofs have touched!

The lamb yawned and closed her eyes. The waters sang all around her. She seemed to hear the singing of the waters with her skin and her bones as well as her ears. She lifted her drowsy head to see the sun and was startled to find it still high above the western hills.

Seldom before had the lamb been so sleepy at this time of day, but seldom before had she eaten so much grass and drunk so much water. Yet it was her head that felt full, not her stomach, and although she had just taken a drink, already she was thirsty. But she felt too sleepy to walk to the brook, or was she too thirsty to take a nap?

The lamb stared through half-closed eyes at the old one as these slow thoughts mingled in her head with the sound of falling and flowing waters. Suddenly she noticed that the breathing of the old doe was dreadfully slow. She watched her chest rise with a prolonged breath until the ribs showed plainly under her hide, and then, more slowly than it had risen, the chest sank down—and down—and down— And then there was such a quiet pause that the lamb thought the old one would never breathe again.

She shook her head and stamped her hoofs against the ground to waken herself. She was remembering the story the old one had told about how the herd had stayed too long in the singing valley and how many of the deer had gone to sleep and never wakened.

"Old One!" cried the lamb. "Old One, waken!"

The old doe moved her head and breathed a sigh, but she did not waken.

The lamb licked the doe's eyes and shoved her shoulder and bit her ears gently, and repeated, "Old One! Old One! Waken!"

The old doe opened her eyes a moment. She lifted her head and said in a dull distant voice, "Who? . . . Where? . . ." Her head sank to the ground and she would have slept if the lamb had not continued to worry and to call to her.

At last the old doe got to her feet, but she seemed to be dreaming. She said, "What is the matter with you, little one? Why will you not let me sleep?" Then she bent her head shakily to the lamb. "What are you?" she asked. "So little and so black and so troublesome?"

The lamb ran in front of her. "Old One!" she cried. "You have already drunk too much of that sweet water! Do not drink more of it! You will sleep again and I am afraid you will never waken!"

But the doe pushed past the lamb and, murmuring over

and over, "I am thirsty," she stumbled toward the brook.

The lamb cried out with all her strength, "Mah-eh-eh! Mah-eh-eh-eh-eh-eh-eh!"

5

The lamb did not cease to cry loudly until the first deer came, a tall buck. He ran around the old doe and the lamb, looking for what might have frightened them, and the lamb trotted after him, calling to him to stop so that she could explain what was the matter. Before she could attract his attention, more bucks joined him in his rushing about. The lamb, run and cry as she might, could not make them listen. And more and more bucks came and they all charged fiercely through the bushes and grasses, farther from the old doe and the lamb.

The lamb could think of nothing to do but run in front of the doe to keep her from drinking the sweet water. She did this so suddenly that the doe fell to the ground. Whenever she tried to get up the lamb pushed her down and cried, "Mah-eh-eh!"

In the middle of one of these cries the lamb herself was knocked to the ground and rolled over in the grass. She lay still until she could breathe properly and then she got up to see what had happened to her.

The young doe was trying to help the old one to the brook.

"Oh, my!" said the lamb and ran after them. "The old one must not drink that water!" By then there were so many deer crowded in and around the place that the lamb could hardly make herself heard.

"What is the matter with you, Black Lamb?" the young doe asked. "Has the madness of man's grasslands come here with you that you wish to keep the old one from drinking when she is thirsty?"

Before the lamb could reply other does had crowded around the old one to support her toward the brook. She was still repeating, "I am thirsty." In despair the lamb lifted her head high, and all her fear and sorrow for the old doe mourned in her cry, "Mah-eh! Mah-eh! Mah-eh-eh-eh!"

Then all the does whirled to face the lamb. The old doe, too, ceased to murmur, "I am thirsty," and tried to see her.

The lamb cried, "Oh, listen to me for a little while!"

The young doe said, "We are listening," and the lamb told them what had happened. Immediately some of the does turned the old one away from the brook and talked to her. Others ran to explain to the bucks what had happened.

But the young doe stayed close to the lamb. "Black Lamb," she said, "you are wise. You are good. You are brave. You are my own lamb-fawn. You have saved the old one of the herd. We will listen to you forever. You are ours and we are yours."

The lamb could not look at the young doe. She hung her head and stared at the ground. The tightness had come into her throat. She thought, Now it is my throat and my head too. They both hurt. I wish the owl were here to explain me to myself.

The young doe said, "Lift up your head, Lamb," and the

lamb saw the whole herd gathered around her. Facing the lamb was the old doe, and there was such kindness and wisdom in her gaze that the lamb felt the pain leave her throat and her head, and her heart sang with happiness stronger and sweeter than the singing of the valley. She forgot the circle of deer and ran to the old one, who bent her head. The lamb licked her forehead. "Are you well now, Old One?" she asked.

"I am well now," replied the old one.

A huge buck with antlers like two trees growing on his lofty head came into the circle. He lowered his head to the old doe and the lamb and then he stood between them.

"Lower your heads, bucks and does and fawns," he said, "to the black lamb. She has saved our old one from the sleeping death. Now she is the little one of all of us, as the old doe is the old one of us all. Will you remember forever?"

"We will never forget," said the deer, and they lowered their heads.

"Shall we leave the singing valley this evening or shall we wait until tomorrow?" asked the buck.

"Let us leave this evening," the deer replied.

At once the bucks went forward to lead the way and watch for danger, and others ran through the valley to make sure that all the deer were ready and to guard the rear of the herd.

Because of the old one the lamb was glad to leave the singing valley, beautiful as it was, but she could not help sighing. "Where are we going now?" she asked the young doe.

The old one answered her. "Our next pasture is not far from the young black leopardess's hillside."

The lamb thought, The old one knows I cannot live with the deer; but she said nothing.

The young doe said, "Drink milk, Lamb, before we start."

The lamb drank milk, but only a little. The milk tasted too sweet. It did not quench her thirst or satisfy her hunger. Nevertheless, she drank as much as she could because she feared that the doe might be sad if she drank none. The fawn drank milk next and he seemed to like it as well as ever. The lamb thought, After this the fawn shall have all the doe's milk. I will drink cold water and eat green grass.

But the lamb's thoughts were braver than her heart, and tired as she was, she gladly trotted beside the fawn, behind the young doe and the old one. Trotting kept her from feeling so sad.

She had a great deal of trotting to do. The deer did not run this way and that to graze as they went but kept steadily on until they had gone the length of the singing valley, out along the river that flowed through the open end, and into a narrow, long, heavily wooded valley. Here they rested a while, but soon they started in the black of the night, through the thick black trees.

Before dawn they stopped near a stream. They drank water but they did not graze, and they stayed close together, moving in a restless crowd among the trees. The lamb was too tired to ask why they were so nervous. She fell asleep and did not waken until the doe had nudged and called to her several times.

6

The herd climbed at a slow slant up the side of the valley, keeping as close together as the dense growth of trees permitted.

The lamb asked the old doe why, and she replied, "Once many deer died in this valley. I do not remember it, but when I was a fawn the old one of the herd told me that the sun came down here to graze. He ate everything, the trees and the grass as well as the deer and the other animals. Not half the herd escaped. The jaws of the sun were so swift and the hot wind of his breath and his red tongue so terrible that many animals went mad with fear and ran down his throat."

"Oh, my," said the lamb. "Does the sun often come here?"

"Never before within the memory of the herd," said the doe, "and never again, I hope. His cloud groves and blue grasslands are surely broad enough, and beautiful."

"What made him go back to the sky?" asked the lamb.

"No one knows," she replied, "but that old one told me he had angered the rain because he troubled their streams, and herds of rain from all over the earth came to drive him away. And so a few deer were saved."

"What is the sun, then?" the lamb asked. "A big buck? A tiger with wings?"

"No one knows that, either," said the old one. "He is too far away and too bright to be seen now, and when he came to this valley he was too big to be seen. The sun is the sun.

His wife is the moon, and their little ones are the stars. Or so that old one told me." The old doe looked sidewise at the lamb as they walked.

The lamb thought of the sun. "Do you think it is true?" she asked.

"No," said the old doe. "It is enough for me to think that the sun is the sun, and the moon is the moon, and the stars are the stars. But it is a pretty story to tell to a little one who likes to ask questions. Do you think it is true?"

"Oh!" whispered the lamb. "Oh, look! The sun is coming!"

The herd had reached the top of the long ridge which made one side of the narrow valley. The ridge was stony, the soil was thin, and only a few stunted trees and bushes grew there. Several lower ridges, like enormous ripples on the earth, stretched gray and somber between the forest and the grasslands. But the grasslands could be seen, dim, empty, full of dark air and sky, beyond the last low hill.

The sky was not empty. One winged cloud hovered over the east like a bird, and below the cloud, below the rim of the earth, the dawn was beginning.

All the deer stood still to look at the east and the light before they went on their way toward the grasslands. The nervousness of the narrow valley left them. They scattered as they went down the hill, and some stayed to graze on the pungent grass of the ridge. Among these were the old doe and the lamb.

As they left the ridge the lamb said to the old one, "That was a pretty story about the sun and I liked it, but I do not think it is true either. The sun is the sun. That is enough for us."

The old doe licked the lamb's forehead. "Come along, Lamb. Let us go down."

But they paused once more at the top of the ridge and looked at the east. They saw sunlight touch the winged cloud and then they started rapidly down the hillside to catch up with the herd.

PART FOUR

I

The day the mad dog drove the black lamb and her mother from the flock their loss was not noticed until evening. The flock had then grazed so far that although he would have given his life to have found those two, the shepherd's third son knew it was too late to search.

The young man had been distracted by his sheep dog after the scattering of the flock. The old dog had smelled the madness of the young one and feared to follow him and his victims, lest he infect the whole flock with madness. The dog could not tell his master what he feared, but he drove the flock away from the madness as fast as he could, and led his master away too. It was a long while before the shepherd and the dog and the flock were calm. The young man never did discover what had scattered the flock and frightened the dog so strangely.

The loss of his father's most prized ewe and his own lamb made the shepherd's third son very sad. This was the first large flock entrusted completely to his care. He had had charge of the fold while the lambs were being born, and his father had given him the most beautiful ewes as a sign of his confidence. Moreover, the young man suspected that the rivalry between himself and his eldest brother was to be decided at the end of the summer by the condition of each of their flocks.

The shepherd and his wife had three sons and one daughter, the little girl who had been so fond of the mad young dog. The time had come for the parents to decide whether their first or third son should be chosen to take the shepherd's place when he grew too old to manage his flocks. (The second son had already been given the responsibility of the farms and orchards on which grains for the flocks and food for the shepherd's family and herdsmen were grown. The second son had always wanted to be a farmer, and he had proved himself a good one.)

The little girl was still too young to choose her work. The shepherd knew he would need a successor before his daughter could decide what she wished to do with her life.

The grandmother of the family, the shepherd's mother, had managed the flocks and farms many years after the early death of her husband and before her son grew up. She still helped in the management, but the little girl was more like her mother than her grandmother. (The shepherd's wife was a weaver.) The little girl was already helping at the looms and was interested in the colors and designs of the cloth.

So the shepherd and his wife had to choose between his first and his third sons.

The choice was easy for everyone except the shepherd. His wife, his mother, his other sons—including the third son—and all the herdsmen thought the eldest son should be chosen. The eldest son thought so himself, but he was careful to let no one know this because he loved his young brother and rival and trusted the judgment of his father. The grandmother thought it foolish even to consider the third son as the possible shepherd.

Ever since he had been a little boy the third son had, somehow, made his grandmother nervous. He often talked about sheep more fancifully than his mother talked about sheep's wool. When he looked at his grandmother there was an expression on his face that seemed a mockery. There was a tone in his voice when he spoke to her that seemed to ridicule her authority and reject her knowledge.

She was a very old, wise woman, loved, respected, and a little feared by her family. Two members of the family loved her more than the rest and did not fear her at all. These two were her third grandson and her granddaughter.

The loss of the ewe and the lamb was followed by other accidents and misfortunes to the third son's flock. Two lambs died. A ewe fell down the steep bank of a stream and broke her neck. Even the sheep dog, one of the best the shepherd had ever trained, managed to strain a leg. When this happened the third son took home his flock and his bandaged dog and asked his father to appoint another herdsman.

The young man told his father everything that had happened to the flock.

The shepherd said, "Son, fine sheep have been lost, ewes

have broken their necks, lambs have died, and dogs have been crippled in flocks other than yours."

"I know, Father," said his third son, "but I can't think of the flock. I think of the sheep."

He had been pacing the length of the room. Now he sat on the footstool in front of his father's chair, clasped his hands together, and looked at his father with the eyes that were so like his mother's. "I love the flock," he said, "but, Father, I'm no shepherd. I'm a lamb and a wolf and grass and the grazer. I can't give my life to the multitudinous. I'm a lover of singularity, of multiplicity. I'm a master fool."

The father and son smiled at each other: "master fool" was the grandmother's name for her third grandson.

"Your grandmother does worry you?" asked the shepherd. "I've never thought she did."

"She doesn't worry me," said the young man, "except in the sense that I love her and that everything I love worries me."

The shepherd smiled again. "What would you like me to do?" he asked.

"Give my flock to the best herdsman and send me out to the 'end of the world.' "

(The folds and pastures where sick animals were cared for they called the "end of the world," because it was in such a distant and isolated place.)

The shepherd continued to smile at his son, but his smile was unhappy. "And there," he said, "you will play your flute and sing your songs and think your thoughts, and you will shepherd sheep that may never exist in pastures too singular for multiplicity and the multitudinous. Or that is what your grandmother will say."

"Yes," said the young man, "and what she says will be true."

"She is an old, wise woman," said the shepherd, "and anything she may say is bound to have some truth in it. But, son, I don't like to see you run away from a fair contest. You should play it out. Whether or not it is a mere game after it is over, it is a fair contest."

The young man smiled at his father, leaned forward, and touched his hand. "Father, I think there's really no contest between my brother and me. You and my grandmother are having a contest, and it has nothing to do with sheep or shepherds."

He watched his father's face closely after he had spoken. He saw there surprise, thought, and finally understanding. Then he saw great love and peace in his father's face.

They stood up. The shepherd put his arm over his son's shoulders as they went out of the house. "You're right, son," he said, "but just the same, I was not wrong. I do love you too much. You are the very size and shape and color of my dearest love. But, son, I understand you too—perhaps not so deeply as you understand yourself, but deeply enough to be sure you could have taken my place as well as your brother, if you had wanted to." He repeated, "If you had wanted to," and smiled at his third son again. "The multitudinous is no enemy of multiplicity and singularity: they are friends."

"Perhaps someday I'll discover that they are," said the young man.

"Well," said the shepherd, "I'll take this flock until you send the herdsman in from the 'end of the world.' Now go see your mother. I'll hitch up the wagon for you."

Thus it happened that it was the third son who saw the black lamb with the deer as the herd ran down from The Children's Grove into the grasslands.

The young man came out of the fenced pastures and the healing folds for an early-morning ride before he had his breakfast and began his day's work. He sat still on his horse while the deer bounded down the last slope of the last hill and scattered through the grass. He was about to ride out toward the herd to watch the soaring leaps of the deer when he saw the old doe and the lamb coming more slowly, last of all, down the slope in the first full rays of the sun.

He could not believe his eyes. When he had recovered from his wonder he tore his gaze from the black lamb and frowned at the tip of his horse's left ear. Then, after a last long look at the lamb, he walked his horse behind a screen of trees and, hidden from the deer, galloped away in the opposite direction. He leaned forward and let the horse run as he wished. The horse slowed to a walk and the young man sat erect.

"I am a master fool," he said aloud, but he did not seem to mind. He took a flute from a pocket and, as his horse grazed and put back his ears to listen, the young man played the tune of an old song.

He finished the tune and played another before he galloped to the "end of the world."

The deer had gone, and with them the lamb. The young man did not feel easy in his mind because, after all, it was his father's lamb, not his. But his heart was happy.

2

The shepherd's mother was thin, small, and stooped, yet she moved and spoke as eagerly as a girl. Everything interested her, most of all her third grandson and her only granddaughter. She was always angry with her third grandson, and she was never angry with her granddaughter. It was chiefly on their account that she awakened early and all day walked around the buildings or drove through the pastures, watching and advising and helping. Although everyone worked hard enough, they all worked harder when they heard her quick feet and cane or the well-oiled wheels of her little cart. All except her third grandson and her granddaughter. These two stopped whatever they were doing as she approached and thought only of her, they loved her so much.

When the shepherd's third son came in from the "end of the world" for clean clothes and fresh supplies of food and medicines, he looked for his grandmother as soon as he had seen his father and mother and made arrangements about the things he needed. He found her about to climb into her little cart for a drive through the pastures.

"You're looking well today, Grandmother," he said, and

picked her up and put her into the cart as though she were a small child. "There was something at the 'end of the world' that made me think of you. A black lamb had been adopted by a herd of deer, and I saw it coming from The Children's Grove with a doe so old she was more silver than brown."

"And so stiff, I suppose," said the grandmother, "that you had to help her down the hill."

"But, Grandmother," said the young man, "the black lamb reminded me of you. It was so little and so brisk."

The old woman turned in the cart and peered scornfully into the eyes of her third grandson. "At least," she said, "you never before made fun of me. I suppose you're feeling bitter about your failure with your flock, and since I'm the only one who's spoken my mind from the beginning, you must gibe at me." She had turned after the first stabbing glance and was arranging herself in the cart as she spoke. She looked again at her grandson. "But why must you go about it in such a silly way? Why must you invent a story about a lamb adopted by deer to tell me you resent my interference in this foolish contest your father is staging?"

"Grandmother—" the young man said, smiling.

"Don't look at me that way," said the old woman. She leaned back in the cart and shook her head. "Do you really expect me to believe you saw the lamb you lost coming out of The Children's Grove with a herd of deer?"

"Yes," said the young man, "I do expect you to believe me."

His solemnity surprised the grandmother into silence.

After a moment of consideration she decided to believe him, and he saw she was excited and pleased by his story of the lamb.

"That's a very strange thing," she said, and her face was young with wonder and memory. "Like an omen, it is. Like the stories of your great-grandfather's grandfather when he was a boy, of the days when his father fenced these pastures. Then a lamb was seen gamboling one spring with a leopard. It was a white leopard." She frowned at her hand on the reins. "I forget the color of the lamb."

Her grandson laughed aloud, not at what his grandmother had said but at how like a little girl she seemed. "A white leopard!" he exclaimed. "That's more fantastic than a silver doe. Do you expect me to believe that, Grandmother?"

"You may believe what you please!" snapped the old woman. One of the things she liked least about her third grandson was his habit of laughing at what she did not consider funny. "In those days the earth was not fenced and tame, not locked up in books and smothered in words, and sometimes it spoke to man in its own voice."

The young man put a large brown hand over the small white hands of his grandmother and sighed as he smiled. "I wish I'd been your great-grandfather's grandfather," he said.

She jerked her hands away and shook her head. "Not even your own blood is safe from you. You'd play the fool with anyone and anything!"

"Grandmother!" the young man exclaimed.

"Don't look at me that way," she said. "I must see this

lamb. Could you bring it to me or shall I go with you to see it?" She turned to him anxiously. "You didn't leave it at the 'end of the world'? Was it in good condition? Thin, I suppose?"

"The lamb is with the deer," said the young man; and added as he saw the shock of unbelief in the old face, "It seemed so happy, trotting down the hill with the doe, I hadn't the heart to bother them."

The grandmother struggled to understand this ridiculous statement. "Tell me plainly," she said, "is this the truth or is it one of the fables you invent to amuse your sister?"

"It's the truth, Grandmother," the young man replied. "I learned long ago my fables don't amuse you."

He was sorry he had told his grandmother about the lamb and the deer. He had supposed she might be annoyed with him but he had not foreseen how angry she would be.

"And you dare to call yourself a shepherd!" she said. She slapped the reins against the fat back of her mare and drove off.

Her grandson's surprise became sorrow, because he had made his grandmother angry, not because he had let the lamb go. He had planned to tell his sister about the lamb, and now he changed his mind. He checked the supplies which had been loaded on his wagon, said good-by to his parents, and went back to the "end of the world."

The grandmother drove a blindly furious mile before she remembered that she had meant to tell her grandson to be sure to see his sister. The child was listless and pale, and her grandmother was worried about her.

The old woman pulled up her horse as she remembered. She sat in her cart, fuming with indecision, but she drove on. She could not bear, she thought, to see her fool of a grandson for a while, and he would return in a few days or could be sent for if necessary.

3

The black lamb did not see the "end of the world" until she had descended the last slope of the last hill. The low buildings and the fenced enclosures were screened by trees. As she saw the place she smelled an odor she had almost forgotten, the quiet cherished warmth of a flock. Her heart seemed to stop beating and then to leap and frolic. She ran toward the folds. She hesitated and stopped. She cried softly, "Mah-eh-eh?" and went on, with softer and more frequent cries.

The old doe watched her, but she did not follow or speak. When she heard the thudding hoofs of a buck who was following the lamb's cry she stopped him. The buck glanced wildly about but remained beside the old doe.

The silence of the houses was broken by the impatient barking of a dog. The third grandson's dog, who had strained his leg, had been shut up so that he would not follow his master's morning ride. He heard the lamb. His leg, the closed door, and the absence of his master, which kept him from the lamb, tormented him. He whined and howled to hear a lamb crying outside the folds, beyond his care.

The lamb stopped as she heard the dog. The memories vanished of her mother, the flock, the comfortable crowded folds. She remembered the mad young dog, the death of her mother, the leopardess, the owl, and the deer. She saw the old doe and the buck, but they seemed far from her. She did not fear the dog, but she was lonely in her memories.

She was distracted from dismal thoughts by a rustle in the grass near a fence and went to see what it was. She cared very little what might be rustling in the grass, but she was glad to forget, if only for a moment, how unhappy she was.

She found a small gray animal rolling in the leaves of a plant with such a strongly aromatic scent that she sneezed. When she looked again he was sitting on a fence post, washing his face with his paws.

"You look like the young black leopardess," said the lamb, "but you are smaller and you are gray and gray-striped and your ears are larger. What are you?"

"I am myself," he said. "You are a black lamb."

"I know I am a black lamb. I have been a black lamb ever since I began," she said. "But you do look like the leopardess."

"I have seen leopards," said the small animal with a large pride, "both yellow and black. They are cats too. I have seen everything. The third grandson has just galloped away on his horse. He saw you."

"Am I his lamb?" she asked.

"Is he your shepherd?" asked the cat.

"I do not like dogs, though," said the lamb.

The little cat jumped from the fence post. "The deer are waiting for you," he said. "Man will not kill his dogs simply because you do not like them."

"Do you like dogs?" asked the lamb.

"I like man," the cat replied. He walked to the lamb and smelled her nose and then he looked at her with eyes as clear as the leopardess's eyes. "I like you too," he said. "Go back to The Children's Grove. You have lost the look and the smell of a flock, but man will be too busy to notice that. Man is very busy always. Even the third grandson carries a hollow stick and makes noises like birds when he has nothing else to do. Man is afraid to be quiet."

"Why?" asked the lamb.

"Go back to The Young Woods," said the cat. "You ask too many questions for a lamb." He ran like a puff of gray smoke blown over the green grass.

The lamb watched him climb a tree and jump to the roof of one of the buildings. He stretched out in the sunshine and went to sleep.

The lamb returned to the old doe.

The lamb could see that the doe and the buck were anxious to get away from that place. They went as fast as they could until they caught up with the rest of the herd. Even then, although the buck left them and they grazed as they went, they did not graze slowly enough for talking. They stayed near The Children's Grove.

The young doe and the fawn came to take their midday rest with the old doe and the lamb. She told them about her talk with the little gray cat.

"You are ours, not man's," said the young doe. "Forget man and his dogs and his cats. We will take care of you forever."

The lamb said nothing. Her heart and her head ached. Her eyes and her bones, even her ears and her tail, were tired.

The old one said, "Do not trouble the lamb, child. She is troubled enough, and tired, and it is still a long way to the leopardess's hillside."

The lamb felt the young doe step back from her and knew that she was staring in astonishment at the old one. If they said anything else the lamb did not hear it. She was asleep.

They did not awaken her until the afternoon was half gone and the herd had once again grazed far ahead of them. The buck had stayed behind to guard them. The lamb was hungry; they did not catch up with the herd until late in the afternoon. The setting sun cast its long level rays against the first hills of the forest. The deer were widely scattered and black against the western light. Their shadows stretched and shrank over the slopes of the grasslands, or moved, enormous, across the gold-green leaves of the hills.

From time to time as the lamb grazed she stopped to look at The Children's Grove to see whether she could recognize the leopardess's hillside or see the white owl flying above the trees; but all the hillsides seemed much alike and none of the birds she saw was white. The deer were grazing farther into the grasslands, but the lamb lagged behind them and the young doe and the fawn and the old one stayed with her. They were almost the last of the herd to notice the excitement of several deer who were grazing along a brook some distance away.

The old doe saw that one by one all the bucks were leaving the does and fawns and running toward one point. She went up a slope for a better view. The bucks were forming themselves in a wide half-circle around a thicket of bushes near the brook. As more and more bucks arrived the circle closed cautiously toward and around the thicket.

The old doe said, "Bring the lamb as fast as you can," and raced toward the thicket.

The young doe said, "Come!" and leaped to where the old doe had been standing.

The lamb trotted up the slope and asked, "What has happened?"

"Hurry, Lamb," said the doe. "I think the bucks have trapped a—a cat."

The lamb said, "A cat?" and saw the closing circle of bucks. She saw the old one, already halfway to the circle. Then she saw a white bird flying from The Young Woods toward the thicket.

The doe was surprised at how fast the lamb could run.

4

When the lamb reached the thicket the bucks had completely encircled it. The does and fawns were some distance away, and with them were a few guardian bucks. There was no sound except the tense angry breathing of the bucks.

The old doe had persuaded them to stop, but they did not break their circle.

The white owl glided above them. When the lamb tried to push through the circle he said, "Do you still wish to die, Black Lamb?"

"The young—black leopardess—" the lamb gasped.

"She would not wish you to be hurt," said the owl, and to the buck with the broken antlers who was beside the lamb he said, "I would alight on a branch of your antlers if you could hold your head still."

The buck held his head as still as he could and the owl settled on a prong of his antlers; but the buck was nervous, and sometimes, in spite of himself, he tossed his head or pranced a step or two, and the owl was several times nearly thrown off his perch.

As the owl alighted the old doe said to him, "The bucks will not break their circle until the young black leopardess shows herself. A yearling heard the snarl as he was about to go through the thicket, but the cat has not been seen."

"The thicket is dense," said the owl. "I can see nothing but leaves from above."

"Let her speak to the lamb or show her face," said the old one loudly enough for the leopardess to hear.

The owl said "Uhhh!" and thrashed his wings as the buck jerked his head. Then everyone was silent, but there was no sound from the thicket.

"It is foolish to wait for speaking or showing if that is the leopardess," said the owl.

"And it is foolish to talk of breaking the circle otherwise," said the old doe. "We will not free this cat until we are sure it is the lamb's leopardess."

The owl said, "She was not on her willow branch, Black Lamb. I told her yesterday you would soon be grazing near her hillside and I have not seen her in the forest all day. Yet I cannot believe she would ever be trapped by deer."

"I will go in and see," said the lamb.

"And if you see a tiger?" the owl asked. "Uh! Uhhhh!"

At the word "tiger" the buck with the broken antlers tossed his head violently and the owl was flung into the air. He said to the lamb, "You and I may as well leave this place."

The circle of bucks was again moving toward the thicket, snorting and curveting.

The owl swooped so low over the thicket that his wings swished in the leaves. "Young Black Leopardess," he said, "once when you were small and hurt and starving I gave you meat from my kill. Show yourself to me now."

The bucks halted. The owl circled slowly over the thicket.

Not a leaf stirred, or a sound.

The lamb squeezed through the legs of the bucks, trotted to the brook, and splashed through the water.

The owl flew at her head and beat her with his wings. "Even if it is the leopardess you cannot trust her!" he shrieked. "She is trapped. She will kill you and not know you, and not care if she does know you. Come away with me. She may yet break through the circle, but this is out of my sphere, and your sphere too!"

"She is not death," said the lamb. "She is only a young black leopardess."

The owl screeched something the lamb could not understand and flew up. He did not fly away but circled silently higher and higher above her, straight toward the sky.

The lamb went on to the bushes. She pushed through the thick leaves and came, suddenly, into a low cavelike space dark in early twilight. For an instant she could see nothing; then she saw, crouched away from her, a dim cat-shape with one lifted paw. She saw the bared fangs of a leopard face, but the paw and the face were spotted-yellow and white, not black.

The lamb kept still, and the leopard too. As the lamb's eyes became accustomed to the half-light she saw that only one golden eye glared at her through the dusk. The terrible gaping face was turned slightly aside, but she could see a dark stain of blood around the more distant eye. As she watched, the leopard lowered his threatening paw and rubbed desperately at the eye. Then, flattened against the ground, he came toward her.

"No," whispered the lamb. "You stay here and be quiet."

The fangs gleamed, the paw unsheathed its claws and threatened the lamb, but it wavered and did not touch her. The dull gold glow of the injured eye was hidden two or three times by the swollen eyelid.

The lamb backed out of the thicket and faced the deer. "You see," she said, "I am all right. You must break your circle now."

The bucks hesitated, but at a signal from the old doe they

scattered. At last there remained on the bank of the brook only the buck with the broken antlers, the young doe and her fawn, and the old doe. Behind them the herd started across the grasslands, the bucks charging in broad arcs to the front and sides of the herd as they went.

The young doe and the fawn said nothing. They looked across the brook at the lamb and tears fell from their eyes and rolled like beads of dew down the blades of the grass.

"Before the next moon has waned," said the old doe, "the herd will be grazing in The Children's Grove, in hills not far behind the leopardess's hillside. The leopardess can show you where, or the owl, or I will find you and take you there. Will you graze with us a few days then, little black one?"

"Yes," said the lamb.

The old doe murmured something the lamb could not hear, and the four deer whirled to leap after the already distant herd.

The owl had alighted on the ground beside her and talked for some time before the lamb saw or heard him. At last she shook herself, for she was still wet from splashing through the brook to the thicket, and looked at the owl.

"What did you say, Owl?" she asked.

"I have forgotten what I said," the owl replied, "but let us go to The Young Woods. It will soon be dark." He leaned close and whispered, "You and I had better start ahead. The leopardess will follow. She has never before been trapped and for a while she will be angry and ashamed."

"That is a yellow leopard in the bushes," said the lamb. "One of his eyes is hurt."

The owl was in the air and hovering over the lamb before she had finished speaking. "I do believe you are more annoying than the leopardess," he said furiously. "Come, come! You are not dead yet. Maybe I can keep you alive a few hours more!" And he swooped down and tweaked the lamb's tail and pinched her legs to hurry her along.

The lamb cried, "Meh!" and kicked up her hind hoofs and started with a jerk toward The Young Woods. Whenever she stopped the owl beat her with his wings and pinched her with his beak, and all the time he scolded her or muttered to himself things the lamb could not understand very well.

Thus they went across the grasslands through the deepening twilight. They had covered only half the distance before the last dim light of day had faded and all the stars of night were in the sky.

"Let me alone, Owl," the lamb panted. "I have to rest a while. I have used up all my breath."

The owl had grown angrier as they went along, not calmer. He alighted beside the lamb, however, and walked up and down, ruffing his feathers, spreading his wings out from his sides, and occasionally standing still and hissing softly, his eyes and his beak nearly closed. The lamb, as she caught her breath, stared at him solemnly.

She said, "What is the matter with you, Owl?"

The owl came close to the lamb. His eyes glittered, whether with anger or starlight the lamb could not tell. All his feathers, beginning with the ruff around his neck, stood out, and his eyes grew larger and rounder. "I am more perturbed than is proper or necessary, and reason tells me—" he began.

But the lamb heard something she had never hear before, like thunder far away, and yet like no other sound. At first she thought the sound was inside the owl and she was afraid he was going to come to pieces or vanish like mist in a wind. Then the owl himself blinked his eyes and rolled his head from side to side, and the lamb could see he had heard the sound too. His feathers sank down. He cocked his head, closed his eyes, and listened. The lamb wriggled her ears, lowered her head, and listened.

"Do you hear something?" whispered the owl.

"Yes," whispered the lamb. "Are we afraid?"

"Are you rested now, Black Lamb?" asked the leopardess's voice, close beside them.

Both the owl and the lamb were too startled to move. They remained as they were, staring into each other's eyes. As soon as the leopardess had ceased to speak they heard the strange sound again, and now they could tell it was coming from the same direction as the leopardess's voice. They went to the leopardess, put their heads close to her, and listened.

The lamb stepped back. "Something is buzzing like bees in you, Black Leopardess," she said. "Are you all right?"

"I am all right," said the leopardess. "That comes into my throat when I am happy. I am purring." The purring stopped and the leopardess turned toward the grasslands. Her ears flattened. Her crippled paw stabbed at the dark.

She snarled and spat and said, "I know, you are following. Go away."

The owl and the lamb turned in time to see the dim shape of a large leopard slink off in the starlight. He went awkwardly, his head on one side.

"He ran a thorn in his eyelid," said the leopardess blandly. "Let us go into The Young Woods."

"Yes," said the owl. "The sooner the better."

Now and then as they went, the leopardess and the lamb side by side, the owl flying above them, the lamb glanced back. Far behind she thought she could see the pale gold wry-necked shape of the leopard, still following. She did not say anything about it.

PART FIVE

I

For several days after the lamb returned to the leopardess's hillside she felt lonely and strange. The leopardess went with the lamb when she looked for grass, but most of the time as the lamb grazed, the leopardess slept or she vanished into the grasses or the trees on short excursions of her own. Sometimes she lay in the sun with her eyes not quite closed and purred. Often she washed herself. She seemed to see and hear everything, whether she was paying attention or not, and she was curious about any unusual sound, sight, or odor. The lamb learned to go with her, very quietly, to see what it was.

The leopardess talked to the lamb, but not much or often. The lamb liked to be with her, because she was not death, but as she grazed or rested or walked beside the leopardess through the forest or the grasslands the lamb would often look at her and feel more lonely than if she had been by herself. The leopardess was there; the lamb could see and hear her; and yet, somehow, she seemed not to be there. This made the lamb wonder if she too were really there. She would have to shake herself until her ears flapped against her head, or gambol about until she was dizzy, or

speak to the leopardess and hear her voice, before she knew
she was a black lamb, in The Children's Grove, with the
young black leopardess.

Neither did the owl always keep the lamb from being
lonely. He talked a great deal. The lamb liked to listen to
him, but sooner or later the owl's talk either made the lamb
sleepy or she had to get up and run away from him, shaking
her head as though his words were a cloud of gnats or a
shower of rain. Occasionally, in the middle of a conversation
he would be silent, staring at nothing, slowly opening and
closing his eyes. Then the lamb would wait until he noticed
her again or flew off through the trees, she did not know
where.

The lamb missed playing with the fawn and listening to
the stories of the old doe. She missed having the young doe
lick her forehead and call her "sweet" and "darling" and
"love." She missed the stir and movement of the herd. The
owl and the leopardess seldom made a stir or a movement
on the hillside or any other place.

However, much as she missed the deer and lonely as she
often was, the lamb reminded herself that it was better to
be a little lonely and quiet than never lonely but tired all
the time. She did not forget that her legs were too short for
the deer and that the deer were too sudden and swift for her.

Soon much of the lamb's loneliness left her. She noticed
things she had not had time to notice while she was with
the deer, and she made new friends.

Her first new friend was a field mouse. She happened to
see him as she was grazing one afternoon in the grasslands.

He was sitting under a plantain leaf. His eyes were fixed on the leopardess, who was asleep.

The lamb said, "What are you, little thing?" She saw him dart a glance toward her and then nothing was under that plantain leaf.

Then she saw him behind a stick of wood, peeking over it at the leopardess. He said without moving so much as a whisker, "I am a mouse," and was no longer there.

An instant later he was beside a stone. The lamb made her voice as soft and small as she could, in hope that he would stay there. "Why are you always in another place?" she asked, but he vanished.

Next she saw his nose sticking out of a clump of grass. His eyes were looking at the leopardess. "All places are the same," he said. "Too big." He went.

Then the lamb saw him flattened inside half a dried seed pod. She whispered, "Have you no home, Mouse?"

"That cat—" he began and disappeared.

The lamb felt nervous. Her eyes tried to look every place at once, and every place they looked they saw no mouse.

From under a clod of earth the mouse said, "—is sleeping—"

The lamb lay down, tucked her hoofs under her, closed her eyes, and kept still, but her ears were as nervous as her eyes had been.

Nothing happened.

The lamb opened her eyes. She did not see a mouse. She got up and looked all around, carefully. "Mouse?" she whispered.

"—on my home," she thought she heard the mouse say, but his voice was so extremely small that she could not be sure she had heard it. Then she remembered all the mouse had been saying: "That cat—is sleeping—on my home," and she looked at the leopardess.

The leopardess had leaned forward and stretched out her paw, and under her paw was the mouse.

"I am afraid you will mash that mouse," said the lamb. "Do be careful not to hurt him, Black Leopardess."

"I will not hurt him," said the leopardess. "I will only kill him."

"Oh, no!" exclaimed the lamb. "Why?"

"He makes too much noise," said the leopardess. "I would like to sleep."

"Will you be quiet, Mouse?" asked the lamb. The mouse did not reply, but the lamb said to the leopardess, "He will be very quiet."

The leopardess, after a brief glance at the lamb, yawned and lifted her paw. The mouse vanished.

The leopardess went to sleep. The lamb watched for the mouse as she grazed but she did not see him.

As they were returning to the hillside the leopardess said, "Do you like mice, Black Lamb?"

"I never did notice a mouse before," said the lamb. "I think I would have liked him if I had had time to like him."

The leopardess said, "Perhaps you will have time," and they walked on in silence.

After a while, although the lamb heard nothing, she felt that she was being followed. She looked back and just behind her was the mouse. Behind the mouse were three young mice, and behind them was their mother.

The lamb was so startled that she said, "Mah-eh!" The leopardess sat down.

"Where are you going, Mouse?" the lamb asked.

One by one the mice sat down too. "We are going with you," said the mouse.

Astonished, the lamb repeated, "You are going with me—"

The leopardess sneezed. The lamb tried to think of something else to say but she could not.

After a silence the leopardess said most politely, "Shall we continue on our way?"

"Well," said the lamb, "yes. Hurry up, mice."

The lamb's heels prickled a little, but soon she was used to the row of mice behind her, on the side opposite the leopardess.

She was talking to the leopardess as they neared the cave and she did not see the owl until after he had dived from his perch and picked up neatly in one talon two of the small mice. He was, indeed, almost on his perch before the lamb heard the tiny shrieks of the larger mice and saw the small ones dangling under the owl as he flew.

"Owl," the lamb called, "those mice are mine!"

The leopardess sat down.

The owl turned on the air as though he had expected to be halted and replaced the mice in their row. He alighted on a low branch and looked at the leopardess, but she was looking at something else. He looked at the lamb. For once he seemed not to know what to say, although the lamb was waiting for him to speak.

"What will you do with your mice, Black Lamb?" he finally asked.

"I think they will do for themselves, Owl," the lamb replied.

The owl looked again at the leopardess; she was busy washing her face. The owl spread his wings but settled on his branch again. He scratched himself under his beak and made a little sound, but still the leopardess did not notice that he wanted her to look at him. He glanced at the row of mice and, after giving himself a shake, he stared as though he had never seen mice before and still could not believe there really were such creatures.

"Owl," said the leopardess, "the black lamb says these mice will be very quiet."

"Doubtless," murmured the owl absently, still staring at the mice. Then he blinked his eyes toward the leopardess and with a sudden shrill sound he darted at her fiercely.

The leopardess rolled over on her back and fended him off with one limp paw. "Ah, me," she said. "I wish I could laugh."

The owl flurried away.

That evening, however, while the lamb was asleep and the owl and the leopardess were away from the hillside, the snake ate the three small mice and their mother. She was sorry, but she had not known they were the lamb's mice. Lamb's mice, she said, were new in the forest that spring, and she coiled so that the four lumps in her slimness were hidden.

"Are you disturbed?" the snake asked, swaying her head anxiously and not looking at the lamb.

"A little," said the lamb, "but I am afraid the mouse will be very much disturbed."

"I am used to that," said the mouse from behind the lamb's right hind hoof.

There was a startled tremor of undulation and the snake slid away. The lamb carefully picked up each hoof, but the mouse was on a cushion of moss near an old root when the lamb found him.

Crouched motionless on the moss, he said, "Good night, Black Lamb."

The lamb dropped to her knees and for the first time had a chance to see him. They gazed at each other a long time.

The lamb's heart ached. The mouse was so small. She wished the three young mice and their mother were sitting beside him, but she thought it would be better to say nothing about them. "Good night, my little mouse," she said, making her voice as small as she could.

The mouse sat up on his haunches and clasped his paws in front of his chest. "I am yours if you wish," he said, "but, Lamb, I am a large mouse, not little."

"Oh," said the lamb. "Good night, my large mouse."

"Good night, little black one," the mouse said, and the cushion of moss was vacant.

2

Early the next morning the lamb started alone into the forest to look for grass. The leopardess was asleep on her willow branch and the owl was a spot of white high in the tree over the leopardess's cave. The mouse was nowhere to be seen. The lamb sighed with loneliness as she trotted up the hill and sighed as she began to graze in a small clearing around the edge of which grew many bushes covered with white flowers just beginning to bloom. The air was dense with fragrance.

The lamb was pleased and hardly startled at all when the mouse said some time later, "There are too many trees in this forest." He was lying on his side in a ray of sunshine, panting after his trip up the hill. "I am a field mouse. I am used to going through. I am not used to going around."

"You could have ridden on my back, Mouse," said the lamb.

"I am not used to that, either," said the mouse. "I feel strange with leopards too."

"Sometimes, even now, I feel strange with the young black leopardess," said the lamb. "She is so quiet. Her eyes look at me like moons, not eyes. Even when I am close enough to touch her she still seems far away. She looks at me, sometimes, and I wonder what I am."

"You are a black lamb," said the mouse.

"I know," said the lamb. "But what is a black lamb?"

The mouse dropped the seed he had been gnawing, twitched, and rubbed his ears and his eyes. He picked up the seed and said, "If you do not know what is a black lamb we had better not talk about it."

"Maybe not," said the lamb, and she ate grass while the mouse finished eating his seed. He washed his face and fitted himself into a crack in a fallen branch so that he appeared to be a strip of light brown bark on the dark brown bark. But every instant or so he twitched.

"Why do you twitch?" the lamb asked.

"I cannot get over feeling strange with leopards," said the mouse. After searching for some time the lamb saw the quiver of his whiskers under the edge of a dead leaf. As she looked at the leaf it twitched.

The lamb twitched. "The leopardess is away down at the foot of the hill, asleep on her willow branch," she said. "It would be hard for you to get used to her while she is so far away. Forget her until you see her again and then you will easily get used to her. She is not death. She is only a young black leopardess."

"I am already used to the leopardess," said the mouse from a hollow in a tree. "It is the yellow-spotted leopard—lying behind those bushes—that I cannot get used to," he continued, from under a piece of bark that had fallen across a stone, then from behind a root, and then from beneath a fringe of fern leaf.

"Try to be still a minute. You are too many places at once," said the lamb. "What leopard?"

"This leopard," the lamb thought she heard the mouse

say, but his voice was so faint that she had to close her eyes to hear it. When she opened her eyes and searched for the mouse she saw a large yellow paw sticking through the flowery branches. The mouse was under the paw.

The lamb said, "Oh, my," and went toward the paw and said, "That is my mouse, Leopard, if you are a leopard. Do be careful not to mash him."

"He makes too much noise," said a voice like the leopardess's voice but deeper. "I cannot rest. He disturbs me. I cannot rest."

There was a heavy harsh hopeless tone in the voice that made the lamb's heart grow cold in her chest. The tightness came into her throat.

The paw lifted and the sorrowing voice said from behind the fragrant branches, "Take your mouse and go, Black Lamb. Let me alone. I must die."

The mouse lay for an instant under the lifted paw before he vanished, and the lamb could not move for another instant. The voice seemed to be vibrating all through the air. The sunlight seemed to have dimmed and cooled.

The lamb pushed her face through the bushes.

The next thing she knew she was lying in a heap some distance away from the bushes. There were scratches in her shoulder and she thought parts of her insides might be broken. The scratches, she found, were small, and when she moved her legs would walk, and she was sore but not broken. She stretched to make sure she was whole and again she pushed through the branches.

The leopard was crouched away from her. A whining snarl

came from the red gap of his throat through the curved
fangs. There was fresh blood around his eye and his rubbing
had forced the thorn deeper into the eyelid, so that its whole
length was sunken in the swollen flesh. The good eye, too,
was dull with pain, and the twisted neck trembled with
weariness. "I do not wish to kill you," moaned the leopard,
his harsh voice higher and more desperate. "Let me alone.
I must die."

"A thorn in your eyelid will not kill you, Leopard," said
the lamb. "It is harder to die than that."

Stiffly, with his fangs bared and the whining snarl still
sharp in his throat, the leopard backed away from the lamb.
"Let me alone," he moaned again, and the branches fell between him and the lamb. She could hear the thud of his
uncertain steps a while, and then the forest was very quiet.

As they went down the hillside at noon the lamb said to
the mouse, "I am sure a thorn in an eyelid is bad, but I do
not think I would be so frightened of it as that leopard is."

"He has a thorn in his heart too," said the mouse. "That
is why he is so frightened."

"I did not see a thorn in his heart," said the lamb.

"No, perhaps not," said the mouse, "but a thorn in the
eyelid is bad enough."

The lamb thought of the yellow-spotted leopard all during
the midday rest. The leopardess had driven the leopard away.
The owl had driven the lamb away from the leopard. The
leopard had knocked her heels over head and scratched her
shoulder, but he had not mashed her mouse. Although she

could not see the thorn in his heart, she had seen the thorn in his eyelid and she had heard the heart-chilling tone in his voice. In the afternoon she decided she would again go up the hill to the flowering bushes to graze.

The leopardess came to go with her but the lamb said she did not need to bother since the grass was so close that the lamb could call if anything disturbed her. The leopardess's pale eyes darkened with the look that made the lamb wonder, What is a lamb? but she merely said she would find the lamb before dark and went toward the pool where she sometimes caught fish when she was tired of meat. The owl was away from the hillside. The lamb hoped he would not look for her. She did not know what the owl and the leopardess might do to him, and the poor leopard was already sad enough. She did not know what she herself could do, but, anyway, she went. The mouse stayed near the leopardess's cave to look, he said, for a cave for himself.

Of course the lamb had not known the leopard would return, but she was not surprised to find him there again when she pushed through the white fragrance of the branches. This time the leopard hardly noticed her. He lifted his head, his clouded golden eye observed her, he closed his eye, and he laid down his head. The lamb saw that she could not bite out the thorn: it had sunk almost out of sight in the flesh. She could think of nothing to say and so she left the leopard and ate a little grass. The grass tasted bitter and it stuck in her throat as she swallowed it. She tried to rest, wondering how the thorn could be pulled out of the leopard's eyelid. Her heart ached.

As soon as she saw the hummingbird she knew how the thorn could be removed. "Oh, bird!" she cried happily, scrambling to her feet and trotting toward the branch before which the tiny creature poised. But the bird had moved to another flower, on another bush. It seemed not to hear, but the lamb knew it must because it did not let her come near. All the lamb's calling was wasted; the bird swung away through the air out of the clearing and was lost in the showers and shafts of sunfall in the dimmer forest.

In spite of her disappointment, the lamb marveled. She thought, It waves its wings but it does not need them. It is where it wants to be because it wants to be there.

She wandered away, calling softly to the owl. She hoped the little bird might listen to him, since he too was a bird.

The owl called from a branch above the flowers. "I have been here since you began your hunt," he said. "Tell me, Black Lamb, what do you want with a hummingbird?"

"Come over here, Owl," said the lamb. She whispered to him about the thorn in the leopard's eyelid and the thorn the mouse had said was in his heart and how easy it would be for such a steady little bird as she had just seen, with such a long slender beak, to pull the two thorns out.

The owl listened, his eyes fixed on the lamb's face, and when she had finished talking he continued to gaze at her.

The lamb waited. The owl often stared while they talked, but this time he stared longer than ever before, and the lamb noticed he was staring *at* her, not through her and far away at something the lamb could not see. She felt shy, to be stared at so long, and turned aside a moment. When she looked to see whether he had ceased to stare she was terrified.

The owl still stared, but his eyes, usually so clear, were blurred and squinted with wetness. Even as the lamb noticed and trembled, an enormous tear rolled out of each enormous eye, slid off the smooth white feathers, and sank into the earth.

The lamb backed away. She had never felt so lost. The forest had never been so strange. Her knees were weak with uncertainty. In the middle of the clearing she glanced again at the owl, saw he had not moved, and because she could think of nothing to do or say she kept very still. Oh, my! she thought. What now?

3

But a short while later the owl's eyes were as dry and clear as usual when he said, "Black Lamb, I have always let hummingbirds alone. They are not good to eat. They fly in the air, not on it like the rest of us. They drink at the hearts of flowers. It is foolish to try, but I will catch one for you if I can. What it might do after I catch it I cannot foresee." The owl closed his eyes and muttered uneasily, more to himself than to the lamb, "They should be easy to catch." Then he flew into a tree at the edge of the clearing.

The lamb went to the opposite side of the clearing to watch. She had hardly settled herself before not one but three hummingbirds were in the clearing, each hovering before a flower within its own pellucid globe of flight. Soon a fourth was there, and a fifth, and a sixth.

The lamb said, "Ah . . . ah . . . ah . . . ," as each appeared. It was difficult to believe there could be one such bird; to see six gave her a delicate light feeling of counterpoised happiness, as though her own heart were a small bird, not on the air but in it.

The owl dropped like a larger and heavier flower from his high branch. She saw him skid to a stop above the ground, alight, and open one incredulous talon. He had not caught a hummingbird.

For a moment the owl remained on the ground and watched the birds closely. There were now seven of them. The owl pursued one of the birds. He swooped in slow curves closer and closer to the bird. As he neared it he made a flashing downward turn. The bird had moved to another flower.

The owl rose to a higher level, floated there, and watched the birds from above. One of them went to a new flower. As soon as it began to drink, the owl was above it and fell like a stone on it. He was so intent on catching the bird that he forgot the branches below. His white wings tangled with the white flowers, and it was only by great skill that he avoided falling, like a stone, to the ground. With ruffled feathers and with no hummingbird he untangled himself, muttering and hissing.

By this time there were nine hummingbirds in the clearing and as the owl finished preening his feathers a tenth arrived. The owl hunched his head into his ruff and stared at the birds. Two more came.

The owl crossed the grass to the lamb, half running, half

flying. He came to an abrupt stop, and she could hear him wheeze with anger as he breathed.

"Black Lamb," he said, "you see how they are. I have tried before, many times, to talk with them, but they will never talk. I doubt that they know how, the silly things; but I will try again. If they pay no attention you must ask your leopard to go away and I will fetch the young black leopardess. The creature does not swim or run or fly that she cannot catch. But you must not tell her about the leopard, and I will find an excuse to send her away after she has caught the bird for you."

"Why?" asked the lamb.

"Well," said the owl slowly, "the leopardess has never yet had a thorn in her—ah—eyelid. If she found the leopard here she might scratch the thorn out herself, and the eye with it. This is her hillside, you know. She does not seem to mind when you bring mice from the grasslands, but a leopard with a thorn in his heart—that is in quite another frame of reference."

"I think she would like to have a leopard here with us," said the lamb, "and if the hummingbird will pull the thorns out of his eyelid and his heart—" The lamb paused. "But, Owl, if the leopard had a thorn in his heart he would die."

"A thorn in the heart," said the owl, sidling, "is not always fatal, although the pain is excruciating."

"What is 'fatal'?" asked the lamb. "What is 'excruciating'?"

"Black Lamb," said the owl, "these birds may all be gone before you can draw a breath and you may never see another. They are harder to find than to catch. Do as I ask about the leopard, will you? After the thorn is out of his eyelid I will tell you what is 'fatal' and what is 'excruciating.' The leopard will be glad to leave his bush if you tell him the leopardess is coming to catch a hummingbird for you. I am sure he would rather have both eyes, even with a thorn in one eyelid and in his heart, than no eyes at all and perhaps no heart. Now. Will you tell him, if the birds will not listen to me?"

"I will, Owl," said the lamb. "The trouble is, I do not understand you very well, sometimes."

"Black Lamb," said the owl, cocking his head forward so that his little beak was almost buried in his ruff, "I have never yet understood you at any time."

He flew to the thickest and tallest of the flowering bushes and found a perch, his head swaying just above the flowers. The branches were not thick enough to support him firmly and he looked awkward and uncomfortable, struggling to keep his balance and trying to talk to any hummingbird which happened to pause near him.

He talked lovingly. He talked angrily. He pleaded and he demanded. He used long words the lamb could not understand and he used short words anyone could understand. He sang in his high sweet quaver and he hissed with his beak almost closed.

He might as well have been silent. More hummingbirds than before were in the clearing and many of them flew close to the owl, but they paid not the slightest attention to him. The lamb could not blame the owl for shrieking with rage when he finally beat his way out of the flowers and the fragrance and flew toward the leopardess's willow tree.

The hummingbirds paid as little attention to his shriek as they had paid to his softest whispers. They went on drinking at the hearts of flowers. Even the lamb could not help being annoyed, brilliant and strange and beautiful as they were.

When the lamb pushed her head through the branches the leopard was already preparing to leave his bush. He was patting at the leaves and earth to remove what he could of the scent and print of his body. He paid as little attention to the lamb as the hummingbirds.

"Where will we find you after the young black leopardess has gone?" the lamb asked, examining his chest as he moved about to see whether she could find the end of the thorn in his heart.

The leopard did not reply until he had finished with the dead leaves and earth. Then, to the lamb's dismay, he flattened himself on the ground before her and licked her hoofs and ankles and rubbed his head gently against her shoulder. "I will not be far away, Black Lamb," he said and left the place.

The lamb followed him through the bushes and watched him slink along the hilltop, his head low and his neck twisted, caution and fear in every step. When he disappeared among the trees the lamb returned to the clearing. She was sad and angry. It seemed wrong for so handsome and kind a leopard to be so discomforted. She thought she understood, a little, why he would bother the leopardess if he lived on her hillside with thorns in him, while the mouse would not bother her. The mouse had said he was used to being disturbed. Leopards, the lamb saw, could never be used to it.

Leopards have to be calm or they cannot be happy, the lamb was thinking as the leopardess came bounding up the hillside. She walked into the clearing and glanced around it. She sat down and looked at the lamb. Her little ears stood forward and her eyes were all yellow, the centers so small they could hardly be seen.

The owl arrived. He perched on a low branch as close to the leopardess and the lamb as he could, and he disdained to notice the hummingbirds. There were a great many of them and they were as indifferent as ever to anything except the flowers. The owl prepared to enjoy himself.

The leopardess, however, appeared to be as unaware of the hummingbirds as they were of her. She opened her mouth to speak to the lamb, but she paused and, lifting her head and turning it from side to side, she sniffed the air. Still sniffing, she went to the leopard's bush and very slowly pushed her head through the branches. Very slowly indeed she disappeared in the flowers. She emerged after a moment and looked at the owl. The owl flew to a higher branch.

The leopardess returned to the lamb. "Did that leopard frighten you, Black Lamb?" she asked.

"No," the lamb replied.

The leopardess glanced once more at the owl and said coldly to the lamb, "Do you want a dead hummingbird or a living one, Lamb?"

"A living one," said the lamb. "Not dead."

Suddenly the leopardess snarled. Her fangs flashed silver in the golden sunlight. Her ears flattened. Her blunt head writhed on her neck. Her tail lashed violently. She crouched, and her crippled paw gashed the ground. Then, flat against the earth, she was deathly quiet. The claws of her uncrippled forepaw slid in and out of their sheaths.

The owl flew to a higher branch.

The lamb thought, She is not death. She is only a young black leopardess; but her throat was dry and her heart knocked against her ribs.

The lamb did not see the leopardess's first leap toward the birds because it was so unexpected. She did not see many of her leaps because all her gestures and attitudes of hunting were so impetuous and intricate. What she saw was a black fog of motion against the white bushes or the tense black silhouette of the leopardess as she prepared for another attack.

It was over as unexpectedly as it had begun. The leopardess was lying on the ground, her head flat on her paws and the tip of her tail making a stir in the grass. The hummingbirds were undisturbed, although many of the flowers were tattered on their broken branches.

The owl, on his high branch, feared for the lamb. Either the leopardess would kill her or she would not, he thought. There was nothing he could do about it except wish over and over as he stepped up and down his perch that the lamb would be killed quickly if she were killed. If the leopardess killed the lamb it would be his fault, he also had time to think as he waited for the leopardess to move, because he should have known better than to encourage the lamb to have anything to do with hummingbirds or a leopard. The leopardess still did not move, and the owl had time to consider hummingbirds and how he hated the silly things. But he hated himself more at that moment.

He had just remembered to be amazed that the leopardess had not, after all, caught a hummingbird when, with another movement also too swift and unexpected to be seen, the leopardess sprang to the bushes and began another attempt to catch a hummingbird. The second was slower and more precise. It lasted longer than the first and most of the hunt could be clearly seen.

The owl ceased to think of anything as he watched the leopardess. He had never seen before, and he would never see again, such swift grace, such beautiful strength, such perfect skill. The leopardess's fight with the tiger had been a wonderful thing. Her first attempt to catch one of the birds had taken the owl's breath away, but this took away from him his very self. He was no longer an owl; he was an eye.

The first hunt had ended in a terrible quiet. The second hunt ended in a terrifying violence. The leopardess sprang snarling out of the clearing and high up the trunk of a tree. She dug her fangs in the bark of the tree and wrenched a long strip of bleeding bark from the trunk. She dropped to the ground. In a convulsion of rage she threw herself down and rolled there, snarling, choking, coughing, spitting, screaming. She leaped at another tree, stood up against it,

and tore at it with her claws and bit at it with her fangs.
Then she fled into the forest.

The owl closed his eyes, huddled on his branch, and
trembled. The lamb sank to the ground, and it was a long
time before her hoofs were properly tucked under her. She
lowered her head to the earth, slowly, because her neck was
weak, and closed her eyes.

"I will pull the thorn out of the leopard's eyelid," said a
small but distinct voice close to the lamb's ear.

The lamb looked with tired eyes at the hummingbird. As
she looked, it swung away from her and alighted on a
broken twig of the nearest bush. It perched there, bright
and still, and waited.

The lamb struggled to rise. She called weakly to the owl
to find the leopard and bring him to the clearing. The owl
heaved himself clumsily off his perch and flew heavily
away.

4

The leopard and the owl returned. The owl flew less heavily,
but the leopard was as preoccupied as before. He stood still
while the hummingbird probed with its beak for the thorn
and he did not wince as it was pulled out. He bent his head
and let the thick blood ooze. He sighed.

The lamb turned to remind the hummingbird of the
thorn in the leopard's heart but the bird had gone across the
clearing to a flower. She turned to the leopard, and he too

was leaving. "Oh, Leopard, wait!" the lamb cried. "There is still a thorn in your heart."

The leopard came patiently to the lamb. "I am afraid it is stuck there forever, little black one," he said. "If it were pulled out my heart would come with it, and all my blood and breath."

"Can you never be well and happy again, Leopard?" asked the lamb sadly.

"I am happy, Lamb," the leopard said. "I hope I will soon be well. Now I must go away, but I will see you again."

The leopard walked not quite so cautiously this time and before he disappeared among the trees he turned to gaze at the owl and the lamb.

"Well, Black Lamb," said the owl when he was gone, "what next?"

"I think you are angry with me, Owl," said the lamb, "and I am afraid the leopardess is angry with me too. But why?"

The owl considered the lamb and her question for several moments. "No, Lamb," he said. "I cannot be angry with you. You frighten me too much. What the leopardess thinks of you I will not even try to guess. You will have to ask her yourself."

"But, Owl," the lamb asked, "how can you be afraid of me? I do not think I am death. I am only a black lamb, and I love you."

The owl left the ground and flew a series of tight circles around the clearing. He alighted on a branch above the lamb's head and shook himself so thoroughly that the lamb feared he would shake his feathers off. "Black Lamb," he whispered, glaring at her, "you talk too much." He threw himself upon the air and flew frantically away.

The lamb sighed and hung her head. She was surprised to see the mouse, with his paws clasped across his chest, sitting on his haunches in front of her.

Neither the mouse nor the lamb spoke. After a moment the mouse twitched, rubbed his eyes and his ears, and said to the lamb, "This forest is too big and there are too many trees in it, but I have found a fine dry cave for myself near the leopardess's cave. And there seems to be plenty to eat on the hillside. Are you hungry, little one?"

Now that the lamb thought of it she was hungry, and thirsty too. "Yes, I am hungry, Mouse," she said.

"Over that way and down the hill," said the mouse, "I noticed some very green grass. There is a spring, also."

"Are you afraid of me, Mouse?" asked the lamb, trembling.

The mouse twitched and vanished.

The lamb closed her eyes and waited for her heart to break. She was too sad even to think, Let me die.

"Of course I am—not afraid of you," she heard the mouse say.

She opened her eyes and saw a leaf twitch. The lamb twitched. The leaf twitched again and the mouse appeared, rubbing his ears and his eyes. "I never could be afraid of you," he said, sitting motionless before the lamb.

"Where did you say that grass is?" the lamb asked. She would have liked to lick the mouse's forehead and call him "sweet," but she was afraid his forehead was too small to be licked and that he was too large a mouse to be called "sweet."

"This way," said the mouse and led her down the hillside. As she followed him, the lamb noticed that all the hummingbirds had left the flowers and the clearing.

"There are so many strange things in the forest," the lamb remarked as they went across the hillside.

"Too many," said the mouse, "and nearly all of them are too big. But you will have to get used to that, little one."

"I am trying to get used to it, Mouse," said the lamb.

For some time the lamb saw the owl very little and the leopardess even less and only from a distance. The lamb would call and run toward her, but the leopardess seemed not to hear and she was never where she had been after the lamb reached the place.

The young, black leopardess is afraid of me too, the lamb thought as she stood on the spot the leopardess had left, and her heart ached so bitterly that she wondered if there could be a thorn in it like the thorn in the leopard's heart. But the lamb had never seen any thorn trees on the hillside and she had kept away from the ones she had seen while she was with the deer.

Nevertheless, most of the time the lamb was happy. In the long absences of the owl and the leopardess small animals visited the leopardess's hillside and the lamb made many new friends.

One day a smaller kind of deer ran across the hillside and several of them stopped to lick the lamb's forehead. They told her that the doe and her fawn and the old one had asked them to look for her as they passed that way and if they saw her they were to say "sweet" and "darling" and "love" to her. They were uneasy to be standing still on the leopardess's hillside, and as soon as they had spoken those words to the lamb they hurried away.

That edge of the forest was full of birds and their songs but they were usually too high and hurried to pay much attention to the lamb. Also, the owl was annoyed when many birds were about and often when some bird alighted near the lamb he would plunge down from a tree and drive it away.

The owl liked thrushes, whippoorwills, and herons—thrushes most of all, in spite of the fact that the thrushes alone among all the birds were often very rude to the owl. Although he did not exactly like them, the owl tolerated the presence of other kinds of owl if they did not stay too long or talk too much.

There was one tiny brown owl who made the lamb uncomfortable until she was used to him. He came every afternoon, perched on a branch as close to her as he could find, and stared at her. Nothing the lamb could say would make him talk, although she asked him a thousand questions and talked to him until her throat was tired and her head was empty. He listened to her. When she grazed away he followed her and found a closer branch, and he stared again. The instant the sun set he flew away.

"One evening he will say something to you," the old owl assured the lamb when she told him about the brown owl.

"Remember what he says and tell me, Lamb." The little owl came every day and the lamb spoke to him as often as she could remember to, but he stared and stared and stared and said nothing and nothing and nothing. The lamb was soon used to him, and when no other animal was near and something to say came into her head she talked to him. At such times he leaned toward her and listened most intently. The lamb always waited for him to speak. But no. Never.

Several times after the lamb no longer saw the leopardess even in the distance, foxes loped across the hillside. At the sight of the lamb, two of these stopped and looked at her. The latter threw down the pheasant she carried over her shoulders and, with attentive steps and her sharp face blazing with curiosity, ran a wide circle around the lamb. The lamb faced the fox all around the circle, not frightened, but not comfortable either. She did not reply when the fox asked her what she was. She did not like the way the fox looked excitedly about the hillside and said, "She must be away from her hillside. She must have been far away for a long time," and blazed her hot eyes at the lamb again.

"I advise you to wait until your young are weaned before you hunt on the young black leopardess's hillside," said a squirrel, running and scolding up and down the trunk of a tree.

The fox growled and ran at the squirrel, but then she leaped to her pheasant, slung it over her shoulder, and raced away from the hillside.

"It is time for her to come back," muttered the owl that evening after the lamb had told him about the fox. "Her hillside is already beginning to forget her." Then, with grave eyes staring through the lamb, the owl said, "Or can it be that you have driven her away from her own place, little black one? Have you frightened even the young black leopardess so much?"

That was the first evening the lamb began to think of returning through the grasslands, along the brook down which the mad young dog had driven her and her mother, to find the flock and the shepherd; but she said nothing about this to the owl. She did not even mention it to the mouse. She waited several days to start because she wanted to see the leopardess on her hillside before she left, but day after day passed and the leopardess did not return.

At last the lamb decided she would have to leave before she saw the leopardess and that she might as well start the next day.

The owl took his midday rest with her and she tried to tell him she was going back to man, but her throat was too tight. In the middle of the afternoon she tried to tell the mouse, but when she started to tell him he twitched and was gone. She would have told no one if she had not been alone with the little brown owl late that afternoon. She noticed him sitting on a branch quite close to her and staring at her as intently as ever.

"I have to go," she said through her tight throat. "I can't help it. I do not like the shepherd's dogs and I can hardly remember the flock. But the owl is afraid of me and I have driven the leopardess from her own hillside. I have to go. I can't help it. I do wish I could understand why the owl and the leopardess are afraid of me. How can they be afraid of me? I am only a black lamb and I love them."

The lamb's throat was so tight, she had to stop talking. The brown owl was listening earnestly and she tried once more to make him talk. She went close to him. She stared at him as intently as he was staring at her.

"Brown one," the lamb asked, "why are the leopardess and the owl afraid of a black lamb? Am I death?"

The owl quivered with the intensity of his staring. He leaned toward her and she heard for the first time his small voice.

"What is a black lamb?" he asked.

5

The lamb went into the leopardess's cave earlier than usual. She had eaten as much grass as she could so she would not often have to graze the next day. She intended to leave the edge of the forest in quietest dark, after the night-prowling animals had gone to sleep and before the animals of the day had wakened. Much grass and a tight throat had tired the lamb, and she went to sleep quickly.

The leopardess came into the cave and looked at her soon after she had fallen asleep, but the lamb did not waken. Then the leopardess rested in front of the cave but did not sleep. She was alert to every sound; occasionally a soft purring snarl slightly opened her mouth, but it hardly stirred the air: the lamb would not have heard it if she had been awake. The leopardess went again to see the sleeping lamb before she leaped to the top of the cave-rock to listen for what she soon heard.

The distant tempest of the first fight, although it was the longest of the three, did not trouble the lamb's sleep or disturb the leopardess. The leopardess merely raised her head more attentively as the first challenging shriek faded into the fainter sighing of the hillside's trees.

At the end of the fight there was a mutter of noise so low that the leopardess felt rather than heard it; then there was a sharply rising scream, broken off before it reached its height; and then silence.

The owl had been as still as his dead branch, but now he could be silent no longer. "What was that?" he asked.

"Two have killed the third," said the leopardess. "He was too small for his brain." Into her voice had come a tone so cold that the owl shuddered as though winter had returned to the forest and pierced him with frost.

The leopardess shook herself and lay down on the rock. The black eyelids covered the golden eyes. The owl too closed his eyes, but the hillside in all its rock and earth and trees stirred with a light wind and seemed to waken and to wait. The lamb moved in her sleep but did not waken.

She did not waken until the two remaining leopards had reached the top of the leopardess's hillside. They saved their breath to move their bodies and made few sounds until the fight had warmed and revived them. Then there was a swelling and bursting cough of desperation as one of the leopards tore himself out of the fangs and claws of the other and hurtled sidewise and backward into a defensive crouch.

The attacking leopard shrieked with exultation, crouched derisively, and jabbed a contemptuous paw at the other to infuriate and distract him.

The leopardess bounded up the hillside toward the fight, and the lamb wakened.

At first the lamb was senseless with shattered sleep. She seemed to be back at the margin of the river near the leopardess's willow tree, the first time she had wakened in The Children's Grove. She smelled the madness of the young dog and the clotted blood of her mother, and she murmured, "That is the voice of death—the voice of death has wakened me." But other sounds from the top of the hill exploded into the cave and the lamb was soon wide awake.

She trembled as each burst of noise struck her but she left the cave and made her way up the hillside toward the fight. She had never heard the leopardess make such sounds as these, but that they were leopard sounds, as well as the voice of death, she clearly understood.

The owl followed the lamb up the hill. He did not try to keep her near the cave; he knew she would not listen to him. He hovered above her, but the lamb did not notice. She was too much occupied with the task of forcing her unwilling legs up the hillside.

The lamb saw death as she reached the hilltop. The climax of the fight came at that instant, and the defeated leopard's final scream was silenced by the triumphant snarl of the other.

The living leopard fell upon the dead one and labored

with all his strength to breathe. For a long time the only sound in that edge of the forest was the clogged rush of air that groaned in and out of the leopard's chest. The lamb, the owl, the leopardess, even the trees and flowers of the hillside, seemed compelled to assist with an easing of their own breath the efforts of the leopard to regain his mastery of the air.

He lay still until he had accomplished this, and then he stretched his paws and, joint by joint, his legs, his neck and shoulders and back. He arose in one gradual and inclusive stretch. He shook himself. He coughed, looked about, and sat down.

The leopardess walked out of a shadow toward him. There was a menace in her light deliberate approach more terrible to the lamb than any of the sounds of the fight had been. "She is death! She is death!" the lamb would have called to the leopard if she could have spoken; but she could not speak.

The leopardess stopped not far from the leopard and said, "This is my hillside."

"And you are mine," said the leopard.

"I advise you to go," said the leopardess. "I will be sorry to kill you. You have fought well and wisely, but not wisely enough."

The leopard repeated, "You are mine," and waited.

The leopardess sprang at the leopard. There was a struggle, exquisite, horrible, and in an instant the leopard was dead.

The leopardess shook her head, her body, sat at the base of a tree which had not been splattered with blood, and began to clean herself of the bloody crumbs of earth and shreds of leaf that stuck to her fur. Her licking and smoothing was interrupted by sighs and racking and exhausted coughs.

As she shivered in the black depths of the shadow that hid her the lamb's heart ached for the leopardess. She did not know why. The young black leopardess is death, but she is the shepherd of her hillside . . . This broken ray of thought cleared the lamb's head of the terror which had filled it ever since she had wakened in the leopardess's cave.

The lamb was wondering whether to wish the leopardess well forever before she went into the grasslands to find her own shepherd, when a leopard came from behind the lamb, walked past her, and approached the leopardess.

He walked slowly and passed so close to her that the lamb's first sight of him was his heavy looming head. She saw his eye, open and clear, but she could also see there was still a little swelling and the gleam of a freshly healed scar on the eyelid.

The lamb saw the leopardess look at her and at the leopard with the only startled and fearful movement of her body the lamb had ever seen. The leopardess did not crouch and consider this time, but flung herself recklessly at the leopard. The fight began before the lamb could breathe or think.

It was plain even to the lamb that the leopardess could not drive this leopard from her hillside, or kill him. He still carried his head to one side to protect his healing eyelid, but he was larger than either of the other leopards and he was rested and calm. The leopardess was as lean as her bones and tired to the limits of her skill.

A terror as hopeless as the drowning blackness of the young dog's madness overwhelmed the lamb. Now the leopardess would be killed or driven forever from her hillside, and by the leopard the lamb herself had helped heal.

The lamb cried, "Mah-eh-eh-eh!" and ran out of her shadow toward the leopardess.

The leopardess screamed, "Go back! Go back!" and, springing between the leopard and the lamb in an arching and contorted leap, drove him away from the lamb and knocked the lamb away from the fight.

The leopardess did not cast another glance toward the lamb. She hurled herself in a frenzy of violence at the leopard and drove him farther away from the lamb.

The lamb ran down the dark hillside as fast as she could, stumbling, slipping, falling. She splashed through the river at the foot of the hillside, found the brook that emptied into it, and ran madly along its bank into the grasslands. She stopped to rest only when she could no longer hear the hideous voices of the leopard and the leopardess, and then she rested only as long as she had to. The terror in her own heart drove her more relentlessly than the mad dog had driven her.

The leopardess fought the leopard until the last of her strength left her. The leopard was neither so rested nor so calm as he had been. He had fought off the leopardess with sheathed claws and guarded fangs and prolonged and circling flights around the hilltop.

When at last she dropped to the ground and, helpless but still defiant, pointed her head at him, he stayed warily away from her. He sat down, but he kept his attention on the leopardess. He cleaned himself of the blood and dirt of the fight. The leopardess remained as she was until he had finished his bath and she did not force herself off the ground and into a shaken crouch until he had walked, very cautiously, quite close to her.

She bared her fangs, stiffly jabbed the long claws of her crippled paw at him, and snarled as fiercely as she could, "This is my hillside."

The leopard took one step back from her. "I am yours too," he said.

The leopardess's eyes darkened. She held her crouch, but soon the strain of the balance was too difficult for her weariness and she lowered her paw to the ground. The leopard kept very still. The leopardess allowed herself to sink to the ground. She made a cushion of her paws for her chin and put down her head. She closed her eyes.

After another hesitation the leopard walked to her and stood close enough to touch her. "I know you are too tired to wash yourself now, young Black Leopardess," he said, "but I do not like to see these shreds and stains on your fur. Let me clean off the worst of them while you rest."

The leopard waited another moment before he began, most gently, to clean and smooth the black fur of the young leopardess.

She fell asleep before he had finished. As she was falling asleep the leopardess said again, fretfully, "This is my hillside."

"And I am yours too?" asked the leopard.

"You are mine too," murmured the leopardess.

PART SIX

I

The leopardess wakened when the sun was bright on the hillside. She sneezed as a dart of sunshine dazzled her sleepy eyes, stretched, and cleaned her fur until every hair gleamed smoothly in place.

She leaped to the top of a large rock behind her. Lying on the rock was a fish still cool from a stream and three young rabbits hardly cooled of life. The leopardess sniffed at them and looked around her hillside. The bodies of the dead leopards were gone. The leopard came leaping up the hillside with two fat quail in his mouth. He jumped to the top of the rock and laid the quail beside the fish and the rabbits.

"These are for you," he said, "and do not forget that I am yours too, Black Leopardess." He sat beside the leopardess and panted pleasantly after his run.

Before he could blink his eyes the leopardess had seized his head. A soft snarl surged and faded in her throat. "I never will forget that you are mine," she said.

Her claws slid into their sheaths but she still held his head with the pads of her paws and she began to lick the leopard's face. He stood still until she finished. She walked around him, looking at the rips and scratches she had made in his hide the night before. Some that were healing slowly she cleaned with her tongue. In front of the leopard again, she gazed at him. "Are you all right?" she asked.

"I am all right, sweet," the leopard said. He sneezed.

The owl waited until the leopardess had finished eating what she wanted of the fish, flesh, and fowl, and had washed her face, before he floated to a low branch and made a little sound to attract her attention.

"I am not the young black leopardess's owl," he said to the leopard, "but I permit her to think I am because often she feeds me well."

The leopard and the leopardess looked at the owl. They glanced at each other.

"What is the matter, Owl?" the leopardess asked.

"The black lamb has returned to man," said the owl. "I thought last night when you drove her down the hillside that she had gone to your cave, but she did not come out of the cave at dawn. As I was searching for her a brown owl told me that yesterday she said she was going back to man, because we are afraid of her."

The leopardess turned her pale eyes away from the owl. After a silence she said, "Owl, I thought she was happy here."

"I thought so too," said the owl. "But it is true, we are afraid of her."

"Yes," said the leopardess and was silent again. She looked at the owl once more. "Is man not afraid of her, Owl?"

"I do not know man well," said the owl, "but he seems to be afraid of nothing."

The leopard's tail lashed like a whip and he snarled high in his throat. "Let us go and see," he said, "whether man is afraid of nothing."

"Yes," said the leopardess very softly, "let us go and see whether all of man's dogs are mad."

2

The shepherd's daughter still brooded secretly about her dog and would not eat properly and worried her grandmother more and more. The little girl was the only one of that busy family who had noticed that her unhappy dog and the prize ewe and her black lamb had disappeared at the same time. She suspected what had happened and felt it was her fault. Since her grandmother was very angry about it she began to fear and avoid her grandmother. The third grandson was called in from the "end of the world" to see his sister.

The shepherd's home was far from the nearest village and doctor and so the third grandson was "doctor" for the shepherd's and the herdsmen's families unless the illness seemed serious enough to send for the village doctor. The young man had learned how to cure the diseases of animals and he had also studied, although not enough to be a doctor, the diseases of human beings. When his grandmother made fun of him for being half a doctor, just as he was half a shepherd and half a flute-player and half a philosopher, but a master fool, he would laugh and say, "I know what not to do, Grandmother. That's a great deal, but I'm afraid you flatter me. It's not enough to make half a doctor of me."

"There seems to be nothing the matter with her," he told his grandmother after he had seen his sister. "She's upset and she cried when I asked her to tell me about it. But she hasn't a fever. Her food agrees with her, even though she isn't eating well. To tell you the truth, Grandmother, I think, and Father and Mother, too, that you're so worried you've made her worry about herself. She's at an impressionable age and she loves you dearly—almost as much as I love you, Grandmother! Tell her how well she looks, instead of how pale. I believe that's all the doctoring she needs."

The grandmother was so sorrowful that she forgot to be annoyed at her third grandson. Tears filled her eyes, and she clutched the young man's arm with both hands. "But surely you can see she's not herself," she said. "And how could I have worried her, my own lamb?" Sorrow choked and tore her and she bent her head so that her grandson could not see her twisted face.

He was glad his grandmother did not see the tears that flooded his own eyes or the sorrow that broke, before he could stop it, into his own mouth and brows. He put his hand over the old hands on his arm and waited until his grandmother looked at him again.

She saw that he was smiling with the peculiar quirk of the

mouth that always made her angry, and rage pushed the sorrow out of her heart. "What are you laughing at?" she demanded, flushed and shaken now with anger.

The young man had not realized he was smiling. "I've been thinking and thinking of that lamb," he said, "the black one, with the deer."

The grandmother's face lost all expression. She stepped stiffly back from her grandson. "You have," she said. "What have you been thinking?"

The tone of her voice made the hairs on the back of the young man's neck prick against his collar, and the chill moved slowly down his spine. He hesitated. "The little thing worries me," he said, speaking with a lightness he did not feel. "I'm afraid I saw my own happiness in the lamb and so didn't really see the lamb. Perhaps it's not so brisk and free as I thought. Someday when things are in order at the 'end of the world' I'll ride along the edge of the forest and see whether I can find the black lamb."

He paused and looked closely at the cold face and the hot eyes. "Do you think I should, Grandmother?" he asked. "Grandmother—" he said again, helplessly.

She had turned and was walking away from him. She swayed as she walked. Her stooped back bent far forward, and her cane struck the ground heavily.

He hastened to catch up with her. "Grandmother—" he began. He adjusted his long stride to her short steps and bent his head to see what he could of her face. "Grandmother, have you been worrying about the black lamb too?"

The old woman stopped. Gradually, with a great and

painful effort, she straightened her back. The scorn in her eyes and the whiteness of her face struck the young man like a hard blow over the heart. Straight as she was, he was still so much taller than his grandmother that he knelt on one knee so that he could look directly into her face.

"You know it as well as I do," she said in a breathless but burning voice, "the life of a shepherd is worth no more than the life of one lamb. Do you think because your father has a thousand lambs you can make a morning's amusement for yourself out of the thousand and first of his lambs? Do you think, because you can't touch it with your hand or measure it with a stick, there's no connection between your father's daughter and your father's lamb?"

The old woman trembled so painfully that the young man put up his hands to steady her.

She stepped back from him and beat down his hands with her cane. "Go back to the 'end of the world,'" she ordered him as though he were a dog. "The 'end of the world' is where you belong!"

Her grandson remained on his knee, staring after her until she had disappeared behind the buildings of their home.

After he had composed himself the young man went to his father. His father listened to him, smiled at him with love and pity, asked him to sit down, and went to a cupboard for glasses and a bottle of wine.

"You seem always to forget, son, or perhaps you haven't discovered it," he said as they drank their wine, "that your grandmother is a very old woman. The troubles and the fancies of the very old are as difficult to understand as the troubles and the fancies of the very young. Sometimes they're frightening, I know, but they're short. You stay away from your grandmother a while and I think she'll forget the black lamb." The shepherd laughed. "The sooner the better! The peace of this place will vanish like the lamb if my mother and my daughter keep this up! I'm no match for either of them, I know that very well."

The shepherd and his son were silent and drank their wine. As he refilled their glasses the shepherd said, "I have it! That was the only black ewe lamb of the spring here, but we could send a boy off to buy one from a neighbor. It would at least relieve my mother's mind of that mystery. She could never tell the difference. You could pretend to have found it and bring it in to her, and she might think you three-fifths of a shepherd!"

The shepherd gazed at his son with earnest attention, but the young man avoided his father's eyes. He held his glass to a ray of sunshine and stared at the color of the wine.

"If you want to, Father," he said at last, "but someone else will have to make the pretense. The troubles and the fancies of the very old and the very young are frightening, certainly, and they may be short"—the young man faced his father—"but they frighten me too, Father. And how could I deceive her! I love her too much. I know she's old, and now I'm afraid she's not—not well. But the truth is old too."

The young man looked at the color of his wine again and

so did not see the smile of pride and love that lighted his father's face before he spoke.

"And all," his father said, "has never yet been well with the truth. You're right of course. Deception's always wrong. But what shall I do? You're out at the 'end of the world.' You don't have to live in this tempest. The herdsmen are beginning to see shadows shaped like lambs and hear ewes crying in empty pastures. They run to tell me when they see deer near a flock as though tigers had taken to grazing in herds over the grasslands. I've always liked to see wild things near a flock. This land was theirs long before it was ours. I hope it will always be large enough for all of us."

The shepherd stared at his wine and thought of his own youth. He did not see the smile of love and reverence that lighted his son's face before he spoke.

"Father," he said, "if my sister's not better in a few days, why don't you send for the doctor? I doubt if she needs him, but he could talk with my grandmother while he's here. In the meantime I'll arrange things at the 'end of the world' so that I can ride out and look for the black lamb. I know it's a fool's errand, but, Father, I am a master fool!"

"That may solve it," said the shepherd. "Shall I mention to your grandmother that you're looking for the lamb?"

"I'd prefer not, but you might tell her I suggested sending for the doctor. She's always liked him." The young man stood up to go, but he leaned against the mantelpiece and watched the small fire with which the shepherd kept the spring chill out of his room. "Father," he said, "you're

always kind to me. Too kind. Tell me the truth now. Did
it worry you, that I let the lamb go off with the deer? I'm
not asking you whether it was wrong, but do you think it
was a mistake? If I could have known—"

"Now, boy," said the shepherd, "that's a question for a
long winter evening, not for a short spring afternoon. If
you're asking me what I'd have done if I were you I can't
tell you, because I am, in fact, not you! I've already said
that lamb is yours, and any other ewes and rams and lambs
you may want." The shepherd rose from his chair, picked a
light jacket off a hook, and gave it to his son to hold for
him. "By the way," he said as he shrugged his shoulders into
it, "your brother told me to tell you he needs those horses
for the plowing as soon as you can let him have them,
especially the mare. How's her leg?"

"She'll be able to work in a couple of days," the young
man replied, "but that gash in the bay's chest is deep, and
healing slowly. I could break in a colt for him before the
bay will be ready to work."

"I'll have him send a colt out to you."

"He may as well send out a pair of them," said the young
man. "He has two matched three-year-olds. The team of
grays is really too old for heavy sod plowing. I'll break in the
colts and he can alternate the two teams this year."

"You're right about the grays," said the shepherd. "Now
saddle my horse, son, while I see your mother a moment,
and I'll ride out with you part of the way."

The shepherd's third son was so busy when he returned to
the "end of the world" that he almost forgot the black

lamb. The colts were strong and spirited, and although they were used to the harness, they had never worked. At first they were sure they would never like to work, but after a few days they were taking pride in the straightness of their furrows and setting their weight against heavy loads as joyfully as they used to gallop over the pastures. When they were unharnessed in the evening they followed the young man with their eyes as they ate their oats and corn in the little barnyard: they wished he would work with them soon again.

The young man was surprised and pleased but not worried when the doctor rode to the "end of the world" and shouted to him from the front of the house. He came out of the garden plot with his hoe in his hand, laughing and calling to the doctor because they were good friends who did not often have time to see each other.

The doctor was a large, red-faced man of middle age, with a gay voice and a hearty manner. Only his eyes, set deep in his head and as sharply sensitive as a bird's, and his hands, which, although large, were as white and delicate as a woman's, showed his knowledge and his kindness.

They talked about themselves and their work and their friends a while, and then the doctor spoke of the young man's grandmother and sister.

He said, "There's nothing I can do for either of them, and you know that as well as I do. Your sister's beginning to grow up, and that's a duel, not a battle. Your grandmother is beginning to die— No. I don't mean she's ill or that she will die soon. Life's the most serious of diseases, you remember. Chronic or acute, it's always fatal!" He laughed at the solemnity of the young man's face. "I see you don't believe in death. Or is it life you don't believe in?"

"The trouble is, I believe in both of them," said the young man, smiling at his friend, "but one denies the other, and so I am left with nothing to believe—unless love is life and loneliness is death and no one but myself has ever before loved or been lonely."

The doctor laughed. His laughter ended as abruptly as it had begun and he looked at his right hand, opening it, closing it, flexing and stretching it.

"It belongs to you," said the young man, smiling as the doctor's startled face was lifted to him. "Your hand."

The doctor put his hands in his pockets. "Your grand-mother is in a dangerous state of mind," he said. "I don't pretend to understand anything about it except that it's dangerous. Finding the lamb or showing her a substitute might give her some peace, but it wouldn't last. She's a strong, wise woman. She's traveled a long way through time, and now she's reaching a wilderness. Few have explored it. No one's mapped it. She's afraid. It breaks my heart to see her. I've loved too, you know, and have been lonely."

The doctor's right hand had come out of its pocket. It lay limply on his knee. He stared at it. "It breaks my heart to see her," he repeated, as though he wanted to be sure his hand knew his heart was breaking. The hand stretched, clenched, and went limp again.

"But I'm sure it did her good to talk to you," said the

young man, also looking at the limp hand. "It always does."

"No," said the doctor. "She's finished with me."

The rest of the afternoon, after the doctor had left, the young man spent arranging his work at the "end of the world" so that he would have all the next day for riding through the grasslands along the edge of The Children's Grove to search for the black lamb.

He rose before dawn, fed and tended to the stock, and rode out in the earliest light of morning.

He rode home through the dusk, tired and sorrowful. He had not really expected to find the lamb, but there had been a foolish hope in his heart that he might see the little black one on some bright green slope or in some dim green shade and that it might leave the deer and run to him.

In a few more days his work at the "end of the world" would be finished for a while and he could send out two boys to tend to the stock and the garden while he worked with his father and brothers and the herdsmen in the pastures and on the farm. He dreaded seeing his grandmother, and yet he yearned to see her: there was still a foolish hope in his heart that she might understand how dearly he loved her and be kind to him.

3

By noon the lamb was far out in the grasslands, too tired to go farther, too tired to remember clearly the deaths she had seen, too tired to wonder whether the leopardess had been killed or driven away from her hillside. She drank deeply

of the water in the brook, ate a little grass, and found a
place between reeds and bushes to sleep.

She slept well and wakened peacefully. She grazed a while
along the brook, lifting her head to look back toward The
Children's Grove and thinking of all that had happened to
her there. The rolling and shadowless green of the grasslands, the broad high blue of the sky, made the edge of the
forest seem unreal to the lamb, as though she had dreamed
it, not lived in it. But her heart still ached.

*Death lives in The Children's Grove, and not one death
only, but a thousand deaths,* the young ewe had told the
lamb before she died. As the lamb remembered, she thought,
But death is a young black leopardess too, and a white owl,
and a tiger, and even deer. Oh, my, and they are all afraid
of me, except the mouse! The lamb sighed. She could not
understand why they were afraid of her, because she felt
sure she was not death. She was only a black lamb and she
had loved them all, even after she had discovered they were
death.

She sighed again and shook herself. She took another
drink of water and turned her face up the brook. Happiness came into her heart. She raised her head to the sky
and cried, "Mah—eh-eh-eh!" and trotted on up the brook.

I am the shepherd's lamb, she thought. He will not be
afraid of me.

4

The shepherd's third son went home from the "end of the
world" very slowly. He tried to cheer himself by looking

about the grasslands and toward The Young Woods, listening to the birds of spring and watching the little animals busy in the grasses. He glimpsed a herd of deer in the distance and rode far out of his way toward them, but they saw him and fled to the forest before he could be sure there was no black lamb in the brown herd.

He checked his horse where grassy tracks branched off southwest from the road to his home. He sat there a long time, wondering whether he should ride over the rolling slopes to the neighboring shepherd's for a black ewe lamb. He could still be home soon after nightfall. The girl he loved lived there, and he thought with a quiet heart of her quiet face. He thought of how her love would lighten his cloudy thoughts like a wind of music and how she and her brother, his dearest friend, would saddle their horses and ride with him out to their flocks to find a black lamb. He thought—

His horse had turned as he dreamed and was trotting down the road he had galloped so often, eager for the long run and the new flavor of the oats at the end of it.

The young man pulled his horse's head around, spoke to him gently, and galloped home.

His home seemed strangely abandoned when he arrived. There was not even the clatter of looms from the loom house or the usual hammering or sawing or filing from the repair shop. He unsaddled his horse and turned him out in the near pasture. He walked through a passageway between two buildings and into the broad paved courtyard on which most of the buildings of his home fronted. The spring bulbs were blooming in their beds. Above the center of the courtyard the new leaves of the giant oak shimmered in the sunlight and birds sang among them, but the yard was empty of any other motion or sound.

The shepherd's office was deserted. The ashes in the fireplace were cold. His grandmother's room was empty, and he stood in the door, looking at the walls crowded with pictures and old maps and records; at the shelves crowded with books and bric-a-brac and old and new relics; at the floor crowded with an accumulation of furniture, including a footstool he himself had made, padded with wool and covered with sheepskin, when he was a homesick boy in school. He thought how ugly and jerrybuilt the footstool was and wondered why his grandmother had kept it so long. He turned his eyes to the massive crook leaning in a corner, with which, his grandmother had often told him, his great-grandfather's grandfather had killed a wolf and driven off the pack and saved his first flock. Pinned against a piece of pink silk was the newest thing in the room, a wisp of hair from the head of his farmer-brother's first son.

The young man left his grandmother's room and tramped across the flagstones. He stood against the tree and shouted, "Where is everybody?" He was cold with loneliness.

"Here I am!" his mother's voice called from behind the loom house. He found her in her little garden, transplanting seedlings from a flat. "Everyone has gone to help out a day on the farm. Everyone but your grandmother and me."

The young man looked away from his mother. He was afraid to ask about his grandmother. He felt his mother's hand flatten against his cheek, cool and smelling of loam.

"Are you sorry you were born, sweet?" she asked, and he could hear the tenderness of her smile in her voice.

He turned his head quickly, before she could remove her hand, and kissed it.

"Oh, no," he said. Then he asked, "Where is she?"

"Ever since you went back to the 'end of the world' she's been driving in her cart each afternoon toward The Young Woods," his mother replied. "Your father had her followed, of course, but she discovered it and forbade it. She doesn't go far. But I was surprised she didn't go to the farm today."

"She's looking for the lamb?"

"I suppose so, but she hardly talks to anyone now, and never about the black lamb." She stooped and lifted a seedling from the flat. As she made a place for it with her trowel she said, "You know, darling, she's not necessarily looking for your lamb. It was out there she met them when they carried your grandfather in from his accident. The grass fire came from there. The southeast road leads to her father's farm."

The young man watched his mother's lovely hands. "I'll go out and meet her," he said.

5

The young black leopardess did not start after the lamb immediately. She ate a rabbit and a quail, drank water, and went to her willow tree to sleep. She knew how long it

would take her to reach the lace of trees and the smoke
on the horizon, and she did not wish to arrive there until
dusk. She was born knowing man lives in the world, she
was not afraid of man, but she had never seen man. The fur
prickled on the back of her neck and down her spine and
her tail lashed when she thought of seeing man, she did not
know why. For this reason she waited until dusk. She always
went in the night to new places to see new things that made
her nervous.

The black lamb and the mad young dog were both man's
animals, and this made her think man must be very strange.
As she dozed and wakened on her willow branch the leopardess wondered how large man was, what color his fur or
his feathers or his scales might be, how swift a hunter and
dangerous a fighter. She thought of every kind of living
thing she had seen, from snails to eagles. Then she thought
perhaps man was like a tree or a hill or the river rushing
and sparkling below her willow branch.

She lifted her head and shook it and stared about her for
a moment. She put down her head, breathed a deep breath,
and wished she could sleep. She did sleep.

She wakened earlier than she need have, because her fur
was prickling and her tail lashing even in her sleep. She
arched her neck, snarled impatiently, and was very still, not
thinking of anything, merely listening to the sounds of the
river and the trees, smelling the dampness or the drier airs
drifting down from the hillside or across the river from the
grasslands.

The leopardess heard the sound of the young doe's hoofs

while the doe was still far from the willow tree. She asked the leopard not to alarm the doe, and he hid himself in some bushes.

The young doe said, "Young Black Leopardess, it is told in this edge of the forest that the black lamb has gone back to man."

"She started last night," said the leopardess. "She went because we are afraid of her."

"We are not afraid of her," said the young doe.

"No, but your legs are too long for her, and too swift and sudden," said the leopardess. "Do not fear the leopard under those bushes. He is my leopard. He will not disturb you."

The doe whirled and leaped away. The leopard emerged from the bushes and stretched his length on a log by the river. He did not speak or move until the doe was used to him and had come back to the willow tree.

"The black lamb has loved me," the leopard said to the doe. "You and I cannot be enemies."

"No," said the doe. She went to the river and drank deeply. "I have never seen man," she said to the leopardess, "but the old one has. She says man has many legs and that some of his legs are as long and swift and sudden as ours."

The leopardess rose stiffly. The claws of her crippled paw grated through the bark of the willow branch and into the wood. "I will go now," she said, crouching and sharpening her claws, "to see man. The owl says man does not seem to be afraid of anything, and your old one says man has many legs. The black lamb is man's and the mad fox-wolf was man's. I think man must be very strange. I cannot think how man is, but I am going to see whether the lamb is well and happy with him."

"My herd will wish to go with you," said the young doe. "I ran ahead to talk to you, but now they will be waiting in the grasslands. The lamb saved our old one from the sleeping death and she is the little one of all of us. We wish her to be well and happy forever. Shall we follow you, young Black Leopardess?"

"Yes," said the leopardess, "if you wish."

The leopardess leaped from the branch. The leopard stood on the log and stretched. The owl floated from the top of the willow tree, and just behind him floated the little brown owl. The doe leaped through the thickets to tell the herd to be ready.

The leopardess stopped on a stone in the middle of the river to look at her hillside. She noticed a small frenzy of motion on the margin of the river. It was the mouse, darting from stone to leaf to root to stone. The leopardess waited until the mouse was still.

"I wish to go with you," he said. "I am the lamb's mouse."

"It is too far for you," said the leopardess.

The mouse vanished. Then the leopardess saw him sitting on the top of a large stone. "I will take care of our hillside until you return," he said.

"Yes," said the leopardess, "take care of our hillside." She sneezed and rubbed her face hard with both paws.

The leopard walked through the shallow water and licked the leopardess's forehead. "Come along, love," he said. "I am yours too, and I will be with you."

They bounded across the river, went through the swampy thickets and into the grasslands. They did not seem to notice, but they saw the herd of deer waiting for them, a long row of bucks in front and the does and the fawns behind them. The bucks reared and tossed their antlers, white rimmed their eyes, and they breathed heavily as the black leopardess and the yellow leopard passed at their swift half-run, half-walk, along the rows of deer and beyond, appearing and disappearing silently through the low bushes and tall grasses, up and over and down and up the rippled slopes.

When the leopards, with the white owl above them and the little brown owl above the white owl, had gone some distance into the grasslands, the lines of the deer wheeled and followed.

The white owl said to the brown owl, "Fly in front of me or behind me or to one side of me, brown one, but do not fly just above and behind me like that. And tell me, why are you with us?"

"I wish to look at the black lamb," said the brown owl. He dropped a little behind the white owl and to his right. No other words were spoken.

Their shadows lengthened ahead of them as they went across the grasslands. The sun sank toward the west.

6

The shepherd's third son walked more than a mile across the grasslands toward The Young Woods before he saw his grandmother, still some distance ahead of him.

On a rise of ground he stood and watched her. She was motionless in her little cart. Her fat mare cropped delicately at the tenderest clumps of grass and moved forward, step by step, as she wished, lifting her long head now and then as though to stare at the west and the hills of the forest as the old woman in the cart was staring. The late yellow sunlight lay along the grass like honey and thickened and sweetened the air.

The young man could not decide whether to go to his grandmother or wait until she turned her cart and started home. He looked all around the horizon and again at his grandmother. She was moving in the cart; the horse was walking toward the hills. The afternoon was so quiet, the horse and cart, the frail back and lifted head of the old woman were so small in the distance and so deep in the quiet of the afternoon, that he was relieved of his fears.

If she's much annoyed with me for following her I'll go back and watch from a distance, he thought and strolled on across the grass.

But his fears returned as he came near enough to see her clearly. Her shawl had slipped off her white hair. Her head was nodding and turning, as a head moves in conversation, and he heard the murmur of her voice. He had never before seen his grandmother permit herself any of the mannerisms or weaknesses he had observed in other elderly persons. Even her bent back was always propped up as stiffly as her arms and her cane could prop it, although it had been injury, not age, that had weakened her.

He stood still again, hardly daring to breathe. The quiet

and the golden light no longer seemed peaceful, but dangerous: he felt trapped in them, like a fly trapped in syrup. He hesitated to return home, for fear his grandmother would see him and think he had fled from her. Yet he hesitated to disturb her solitude and speech.

As he hesitated she turned to him. She motioned him to her and he ran.

When he reached the cart she did not speak. She simply rested her dark gaze on his face without surprise or interest—almost, he feared, without recognition. Her face was whiter and sharper than it had been the last time he had seen her. Her eyes were as large and as wide open as ever, but their brightness seemed to have dulled or to have sunk deeper into her head.

The silence continued, and the young man could think of no words strong enough to break it. His grandmother's indifference was far more terrible to him than her contempt or her anger had ever been. He wished she would scold him or call him a fool and laugh at him or beat him with her cane or her scorn. He felt a silly smile disfigure his face. He blushed.

"So you've come back from the 'end of the world,'" she said. "Help me out of my cart. I want to walk a little."

He lifted her out of the cart, steadied her until she had braced and balanced herself against her cane. She walked away from him without a word or a glance. She walked with great difficulty for several steps and then, as though she had remembered how to walk, went on steadily. She had not gone far before her head began again to nod and turn and he could hear the haunted murmur of her voice. She had already forgotten him.

Sweat chilled the young man's forehead, and his throat dried and ached. He went after his grandmother and walked beside her, but he did not dare to look at her.

"Grandmother," he said, "I spent a whole day searching for the black lamb. I didn't find it, but I didn't find traces of its death, either. It must be somewhere around here, in the forest or in the grasslands. Sooner or later one of us will surely see it and bring it in."

The murmur of his grandmother's voice had stopped as he spoke and she nodded when he finished, but there was no other sign that she had been listening and soon her old voice again murmured its lonely speech; her white head nodded and turned.

". . . I know how it is with them. They don't have to tell me; I know all about it. But they shouldn't make light of it, and why don't they tell her the truth? They're not telling me the truth, either. You did. I haven't forgotten that. But she is afraid of me. But how could she be afraid of me? . . ."

By concentrating all his attention and bending his head to hers as closely as he dared, the young man could understand that much of what she was saying before it became too confusing for him to follow. The voice had the tone and inflections, but not the quality, of his grandmother's vivid voice. It was like hearing a fine melody played without skill on a cheap instrument. His ears rejected it and his mind shrank from it. He tried to close himself within himself, to escape this mockery of his love that tottered and twittered beside him.

The young man continued to walk beside his grandmother for an immeasurable length of time and space. His hand was ready to support her when she faltered and at intervals and at random he said, "It's warm for the middle of spring," or, "They must be making a good start at the farm," or, "Don't you think the south section should be limed this year?" But he had ceased to exist for the old woman, and by a merciless pressure of will he too extinguished himself.

When he heard the cry of the lamb it was as though he were awakening from a long sleep. He heard next, behind him, the wheeze of fright and the clatter of the little cart as the mare galloped homeward.

He saw the black lamb at the same instant that he heard his grandmother say in an oddly flat tone, "Aaaaaah—" Then he saw the approaching and halting shadows of the deer, with a large and a small bird above them.

Then he saw the two leopards. First the yellow one and finally, black in a dark deer-shadow, the black one.

7

A few of the deer reared and snorted as the young man looked at them, and the whole broad arc encircled them.

The black lamb lifted her head, cried, "Mah—eh?" and came hesitantly toward them.

The young man could see out of the corners of his eyes that his grandmother had straightened her back and was standing at her full height. He sensed her glance flick toward him as his flicked toward her. Neither moved, but each could feel the other's attention stretched between them as tangibly as though they had clasped hands.

The old woman said in a clear voice, "Go back. Go quietly. I'll distract them and you'll be far enough away to outrun them."

He knew she intended to lift her cane and go toward the leopards. "Don't move!" he commanded.

The lamb had stopped as they spoke and now she cried again and came a little closer.

The young man said, "Ah, Lamb—ah, Lamb," and the lamb came almost to his feet.

The grandmother said, "Have you your knife?"

"Yes," replied the young man.

"Get it out," said the old woman, "and when she comes close enough cut her throat and throw her toward the leopards. Not too far, just a few feet. Then run. Probably they won't pay any more attention to me. I'll go back as fast as I can and you'll be able to return for me before they've finished with the lamb. Get out your knife. Have it ready. Do it quickly. Don't let the lamb make a noise if you can manage it. And run. Don't hesitate. Turn and run."

"Don't move until I tell you to move," said the young man.

There was a silence as deep and broad and high as death. In the silence the lamb came directly to the young man, lifted her head to him, and made another soft sound of inquiry.

The young man said, "Ah, little black one," and took the lamb in his arms.

As he did this he saw the black leopardess's neck arch, saw her tail lash violently, and heard a low but prolonged snarl. The yellow leopard moved up to the black one. The deer pranced nervously closer, entirely surrounding them, and a doe pushed her way through the line of bucks and came out within a length of the leopards. The two owls, which had been floating above the deer, glided toward the young man and his grandmother and settled on the ground beside the leopards. The large white owl ruffed his feathers and paced back and forth, always with his eyes on them. The tiny brown owl fluttered beyond the leopards, alighted again, and stared.

It was this action of the two birds that most nearly broke the self-control of the old woman and the young man. A strangling terror flooded upward in both of them. The young man heard his grandmother's sighing expulsion of breath, but he did not hear his own harsher moan.

"Can't you kill it?" asked the old woman. "No. Give me your knife. You hold its head up and I'll cut its throat."

"Don't move until I tell you to move!" cautioned the young man.

He stroked and murmured to the lamb while the terror ebbed from his brain. He compelled himself to stand quite still until he was sure he could control his muscles and move as steadily and quickly as might be necessary. Then he took one step toward the leopards.

The deer reared and snorted and made the ground thunder under their hoofs. The leopards and the owls did not move. He took another step. The black leopardess snarled softly but still did not move. The leopard, who was half a length behind the black one, moved up until his head was at her shoulder.

The young man said, "Grandmother, turn around and start back. Slowly."

"I'll do no such thing, you young fool!" snapped his grandmother. He heard her voice soften, although it was by no means cleared of her impatience, and it surprised him very much to feel the taut muscles of his face loosen in a smile. "Try for once in your life," the strong old voice commanded, "to use the sense you must have been born with. This is no time for heroism. Your father and your mother need you. I have had my share of life. Give me the knife."

"Grandmother," said the young man, "I need you. And I'm sure neither of us is in danger. Those leopards wouldn't have turned their backs on a herd of deer if they were hungry."

"They're afraid of us," said his grandmother fiercely.

"They're not half so afraid of us as we are of them," said the young man, laughing aloud at the ferocity of his grandmother.

After a moment his grandmother said, "We'll both turn at the same time, then."

"You won't turn back?" he asked.

"Not if you don't," she said.

"Now," said the young man. "Turn."

By the time they were able to force themselves to turn again and look back the leopards and the owls were gone, and although they could still hear and feel in the earth the plunging weight of the herd, the deer were invisible in dusk and distance.

The young man and the old woman gazed at each other with the blank eyes of exhaustion. The young man put his face against the lamb's head and said, "Are you all right, my little black one? Will you follow me the rest of the way home?"

He placed the lamb on the ground and picked up his grandmother.

"The lamb is following," she said with satisfaction as he strode homeward.

"I knew she would," said the young man. "Are you all right, Grandmother?"

"Of course I'm all right," said the old woman peevishly.

The young man began to sing as he walked, and as he sang he thought, Can I ever be this happy again? Already it's leaving me. Already it's beginning to fade. Farewell. Farewell—

He felt the light small body move impatiently in his arms. "Do stop that noise," said his grandmother. "I want to say something to you." He stopped. "What are we going to tell them?" she asked.

"Why—!" exclaimed the young man. "There is only one thing to tell." He tried to see his grandmother's face clearly through the dusk.

"Everybody thinks you're a fool," she said, "but if I began

to tell such tales the place would turn into a madhouse. It would be better to say it was a wolf."

"But, Grandmother, there are no wolves near here. They've all been killed or driven to the mountains or bred into dogs—"

"It's not impossible that a wolf could have strayed down from the mountains."

"Grandmother," said the young man, "it was a stray wolf. Are you coming, little black one?"

"Mah-eh-eh-eh-eh!" cried the lamb.